BLUE HYDRANGEAS

JJ WALLINGFORD

Bella
BOOKS

2014

Bella Books, Inc.
P.O. Box 10543
Tallahassee, FL 32302

Printed in the United States of America on acid-free paper.

First edition: *Devan's Story: Blue Hydrangeas*, by JJ Wallingford, 2012

First Bella Books Edition 2014

Editor: Cath Walker
Cover Designer: Sandy Knowles

ISBN: 978-1-59493-420-9

About the Author

It took JJ Wallingford, a native Seattleite, several years to finally determine a lab setting and Texas were not for her. With the encouragement of friends and family, especially her beloved partner, this reformed microbiologist relocated back to Washington to try her hand at writing. When not hunched over her computer, JJ likes to spend her days traveling, hiking, camping, snuggling on the couch with her much loved Boston terrier, and enjoying life with her partner and daughter.

Dedication

I want to dedicate this book to my beloved. Thank you for your support in life and with our many endeavors. Everything I have is because of you. Thanks for helping me become a better person. I love you, Janet.

Acknowledgments

I would like to thank Vik Mauro for her invaluable insights into the mind of a police officer. Thank you, my friend. I would also like to thank Dr. Wendy Vannoy for being not only a good friend but a reader extraordinaire. Thank you for reminding me how important humor is in all aspects of life. Thanks to Jesse, my favorite kid, for just being you. Thanks for being a great daughter, funny and sarcastic, loving and loyal. And lastly, but not leastly, I want to thank Mary O'Connell for providing medical insight and for giving life to an amazing human being. Everyone needs a Desi in their life, thank you for providing my daughter an awesome best friend.

CHAPTER ONE

"What can I get you, ma'am?" The bartender asked with a small smile on her face.

Ouch. Ma'am? I was only thirty-six, when did I become a ma'am? "A vodka tonic please. Double." I never knew what to order. I wasn't much of a drinker. I drank Jack Daniels and Diet Coke on the rare occasion I drank at home, but the first time I ordered a Jack and Diet the bartender gave me such a look of disdain I hadn't done so since. A vodka tonic sounded cool and refreshing, just the kind of drink I needed after an unseasonably hot early spring day in Fort Worth.

"Here you go. Anything else I can do for you?" the bartender asked.

"No, I don't believe so."

"If you need anything, anything at all, my name is Kendall."

"Thank you, Kendall." I took a sip, and Kendall smiled and moved to the end of the bar where two women and a man were drinking. I thought they may have been there for the same teachers' conference I was attending. There were so many people at the conference and I was having a hard time keeping all the faces and names together.

When I volunteered to attend this year it had seemed like such a good idea at the time. Getting away for a few days and exploring Fort Worth, a city I had never visited. But the conference was more than I had bargained for, leaving me with very little time to explore. The meetings started at eight a.m. and continued until six p.m. Lunch was provided, but I'd eaten dinner at Subway and Chipotle, right around the corner, and had a drink or two in the bar next to the hotel.

"Can I get you anything to eat, ma'am?" It was pretty crowded. The Thursday night crowd was apparently getting a jump on the weekend, but Kendall managed to stay close.

"Please, call me Devan. Do *not* call me ma'am."

"Okay, Devan, can I get you anything?"

"No, I'm fine, thanks."

"Well, if you change your mind, the burgers here are pretty good and the French dip, surprisingly, is excellent."

"I'll let you know." A French dip was tempting, but back in the room I did have leftovers I hated to throw out. I'd finish my drink and see how I felt. I looked around to see that all the seats at the bar were filled, except the two on either side of me. I've always thought I must give off a strong "don't mess with me" vibe when I go to bars, because this was not the first time I'd noticed the phenomenon. Not that I spend a lot of time in bars.

"Hi, I'm Tom. Can I buy you a drink?" The man at the end of the bar had sat down next to me when I was lost in my vodka tonic.

"That's very thoughtful of you, Tom, but this will probably be my only drink tonight. I still have a full day of meetings scheduled for tomorrow and then I fly back home."

"Can I buy you dinner, then?" He seemed pleasant enough. He wore an expensive older suit, and a tie, which he had pulled down so he could unbutton the top button on his shirt. Salt-and-pepper hair, gentle eyes and a warm smile.

"Thanks, but I've already eaten." He was definitely one of the retreat attendees. I remembered seeing him around, always smiling and friendly looking. "I just came over to have a quick drink before I head back to my room."

He checked his watch and frowned. "It's only eight thirty. Do you want to go see a movie?"

I always disliked these awkward situations. How do you say "no, I'm not interested," and be friendly and casual at the same time? I guess I could just tell him I was gay, but sometimes that wasn't a deterrent. A couple of times, when I told a man I was gay, "gay" to him was code for "let's have a threesome." I didn't think we worked in the same school district, so telling him I was gay probably wouldn't be too revealing. I wasn't ready to be revealing, though. "No, thanks, I think I'll just finish this drink and go read a little." I smiled to show him no hard feelings. I just wasn't available.

"Okay. Could I get your phone number so I can call when you're not too tired and busy?"

"You're very persistent. I'll have to decline, though." He didn't seem to be taking my hints.

"Is there something about me you don't like?" He was changing from kind and interesting to a bit desperate and lonely. Alcohol can do that to some people.

"Look, I'm trying to be friendly here, Tom, but you're making this very hard. I'm in a relationship and I can't go out with you."

"Oh, well, why didn't you just say that?" He seemed a little annoyed, like I could have handled this situation better.

"I didn't think I had to. I was trying to be subtle. I'm not interested."

"Here's my number in case your situation changes." He left me sitting there holding his business card, the card I would never use, the card he hoped would miraculously change my mind. I shook my head and looked up into Kendall's smiling eyes.

"Would you like me to throw that away for you?"

"Is he gone?"

She looked around and nodded. I handed it to her and she discreetly threw it into the trash located out of sight under the bar.

Laughing, I just had to ask. "Why do some men do that?"

She shook her head. "I don't know, honestly. I think maybe they've seen too many movies and read too many books about the guy who chases after the unwilling girl, is so persistent the girl caves, and they live happily ever after."

"You must get that a lot, Kendall."

"Why do you say that?"

"Well, you work in a bar, you're beautiful and you're not wearing a ring."

"In that case, you must have that happen to you all the time. You're one of the most beautiful women I've ever seen." Kendall leaned against the bar and whispered to me, "I get off at ten, if you want to talk later." She pushed herself back from the bar and walked away.

Oh my. I *had* to get out of that bar. I drank the last of my vodka tonic and walked the few steps to my hotel. I must say, the night did wonders for my self-esteem. I was thinking Steph and I had been in a rut for a while, and the thought of someone, actually *two* someones, a man *and* a woman, finding me attractive made my already big head grow just a little bit more.

I laughed at my egotistical self as I unlocked the door to my hotel room, threw my purse on the bed and kicked off my shoes. Wanting to look deep into my eyes I searched out the mirror. Kendall's offer to talk was intriguing and very tempting. I would never cheat on Steph but talking wasn't against the rules, now was it? Was Kendall serious about talking or did she want something more? My head felt a little fuzzy. Was this the vodka or something else?

"Stop thinking about Kendall," I said to the mirror. "You are with Steph." I am with Steph but we had been drifting apart the last year or so. No reason to think about cheating. I jumped a little at the thought and walked away from the mirror. I sat down on the bed and looked around the room. The clock on the nightstand said it was almost nine o'clock. Not very long until ten.

I jumped up from the bed, deciding I needed a little food to soak up the strong alcohol coursing through my system. I ate my leftovers and settled into the armchair to watch whatever happened to be on HBO at that moment. I swore to myself I would not, under any circumstance go back to the bar at ten.

At nine fifty-nine, I found myself walking into the Dusty Saloon and taking a seat at the far end of the bar. Kendall noticed me after a couple of moments and a slow smile spread across her face. She walked slowly toward me, placed a bottle opener on the counter in front of me and said a quiet hi.

"I have a girlfriend," was apparently the appropriate thing for me to say at the moment.

"Okay. I'm a Libra. Your turn, Devan."

"I'm not sure why I came back." I really did have a serious pact with myself to stay in the room. I don't even listen to me.

"Let's see. How about you're lonely and just want to talk to a friendly person? Someone who isn't going to try to get you into bed and take advantage of you?" Kendall took a couple steps back, her eyes never leaving mine, and grabbed her bag from behind a giant can of olives.

"Oh. You're not?" I wondered out loud.

"Do you want me to?" Kendall's smile just got a little wider revealing a slight gap in her front teeth I hadn't noticed before. Adorable.

"No! Of course not! I have a girlfriend back in Austin."

"Does this girlfriend have a name, Devan?"

"Um…" Why can't I remember her name? What is wrong with me? "Steph…her name is Steph. What did you put in that drink you gave me?"

"It's a secret family recipe but I think I can let you in the know." Kendall came around the bar and sat in the stool next to mine. "Come closer, Devan."

I leaned over and placed my ear next to her mouth. She said, "It's a mixture of vodka…and tonic."

I pulled back into an upright position and said, "That's not funny."

"Yes it was. Come on, Devan, let's go."

"Where are we going?" I'm not sure what I'm doing but I'm pretty sure I should be doing it surrounded by witnesses.

"Let's go for a drink," she said as she swiveled around and stood up. She's a couple inches taller than me and in much better shape with long brown hair, dark eyes and dark skin. "I can't drink in the same bar where I work. It's generally not a good idea to mix the two."

We ended up in a bar a few blocks away.

"I like coming here after work sometimes. It's very quiet here," Kendall said as we sat at a booth in the far corner of the bar. A waitress came over and greeted Kendall warmly, took our orders and left us alone. "What do you do for fun, Devan?"

"Well, right now I'm an art teacher at Zilker Middle School, my third year, but I used to be a therapist."

"That doesn't sound like fun." Kendall had a way of flipping her hair back when she laughed I found intriguing.

"Oh right. Fun. I love to paint landscapes and draw a wide variety of subjects with charcoal. I enjoy music and going to see movies and plays. I love being near the water, not in it but near it. What about you, Kendall?" I couldn't think of anything else I liked. I don't think anyone has ever asked me what fun things I liked to do.

"I enjoy sleeping in, hiking, rollerblading, movies, eating and talking with beautiful women."

"Really? Rollerblading? That seems like a lot of work." I thought I'd skip the beautiful women comment. I didn't want to give Kendall the wrong impression of our interlude. I think I gave her the wrong impression when I showed up at ten.

"It is but I enjoy it." The waitress brought our drinks and Kendall took a sip of her vodka tonic. "Tell me about Steph."

"Steph and I have been together for about five years now. She's an intelligent, thoughtful, energetic woman. We live on the east side of Austin and she's a real estate broker. She's ten years older but we really don't notice the difference. What about you? Are you seeing anyone?" I had to look away from Kendall. The vodka tonic in front of me was the next best option.

"Not really. I think I'm due for a change of scenery. I like Fort Worth but the heat is starting to get to me. Maybe New Mexico would be a better fit. Does Steph treat you well?"

"Yes, she does. It's not like it used to be, our relationship. It was very intense in the beginning. She's the only woman I've ever been with, after dating men throughout school. The last year or so has been different." I looked up at her then and found her dark eyes. "I can't believe I'm telling you all this."

"Don't worry, I get that all the time. It's the bartender in me. People want to tell me their deep dark secrets. Keep going, I'm hoping your secrets will be dark and sordid."

"I don't have any deep dark secrets, Kendall."

"We all have deep dark secrets, Devan."

"What's yours?"

"That's definitely not something I can tell you after only one drink. Can I order you another?" Kendall leaned back to look for our waitress but stopped when I grabbed her wrist.

"I really shouldn't drink anymore. I have an early morning meeting. I need to go back to the hotel and sleep." I let go and immediately missed her warmth. "That's what I miss the most about Steph."

"What? Your early morning meetings?" Kendall said.

"No. I miss her warmth. She's gotten colder lately."

"Well, Devan. If you find yourself needing some warmth please give me a call." Kendall slid a piece of paper over to me filled with her name, phone numbers and email.

"When did you write all this down?" I asked because I didn't notice her taking notes.

"After you left." She laid a twenty on the table and stood up.

"How did you know I'd come back?" I stood up and we walked outside into the still-hot Texas evening.

"I didn't. I had high hopes, though. I still do." Kendall walked me to the hotel, said a gentle goodbye and walked away leaving me with conflicting feelings. The vodka wasn't helping. I have never cheated on anyone I was dating, ever, but at this moment I thought about it. Kendall was everything Steph wasn't: warm, gentle and very exciting. I could have called her back, I could still see her from here, but I didn't. Sharing information was one thing, but sharing my body was something entirely different.

The hallway to my room floated by, the bathroom accepted me into its depths and the bed lent me a level of comfort I desperately needed. I spent a long time searching for answers in the ceiling. How could I even think these things? I know the difference between right and wrong and these thoughts were very wrong. When Mr. Sandman finally took over, when I dropped off into a fitful sleep, I dreamt chaos and anarchy.

CHAPTER TWO

Friday was a long and slow day with the "best" presenters saved for the end. I had trouble staying awake. I'd stayed up way too late the night before and I was happy when the last speaker was finally finished. I had checked out first thing that morning and was now sitting in my rental car, ready to go to the airport, when my phone rang. It was the airline telling me that my flight had been delayed about ninety minutes. I wouldn't get into Austin until much later than anticipated.

"Hello?" Steph sounded like she'd been sleeping.

"Hi, babe. My flight's been delayed and I won't get in until after ten tonight. Do you want to pick me up or should I get a cab?"

"Um…why don't you get a cab? That's kind of late."

"Will you wait up for me?"

"I'll try, Devan, but you know how I am."

"Steph, it would be really great if you waited up for me." I hesitated, before saying "I think we should talk."

"Oh, okay. I'll try. Talk to you later." The silence was very loud in my ear.

We really *did* need to talk. We were growing apart and it alarmed me. It seemed we were going through the motions now after five years together, and I wasn't comfortable with just the motions. I wanted more from Steph, more from our relationship. I thought maybe if we talked and I told her how I was feeling, we could work it out.

My time with the intriguing Kendall had made me realize how much my relationship with Steph had deteriorated. I still had the piece of paper with Kendall's information on it in my left front pocket, still warm and inviting. I had no plans to call her but the thought of talking with her again left me feeling light-headed. As I drove slowly to the airport, I pondered what life would look like without Steph.

If I confronted her with my unhappiness, would I be willing to leave? Could I leave? I'd never really lived on my own. I went from my parents' house in Federal Way, Washington to the dorm room, living with other poor students during my psychology post-grad years and beyond, and then on to living with Steph. I'm sure I could do it, but I'd just never really thought about it before.

I didn't want to leave Steph. We had such a wonderful relationship in the beginning. Why couldn't we go back to the golden days? She had been pulling away from me more and more and it was leaving me feeling unfulfilled and longing. I realized that Kendall was right. I was a lonely woman. There's nothing lonelier than being in an unfulfilling relationship.

As I wound around the entrance to the airport, I realized I would probably feel better if Steph was interested in going to therapy with me. One of my worst flaws, and as Steph likes to point out I have many, is my need to analyze everything. I keep telling her I can't help it, after so many years of schooling and then actual therapy it's hard to view the world in any other way. Steph believes therapy is for the weak and won't even entertain the thought of going to talk to a stranger about her problems. I don't know why she would even date a therapist, let alone live with one, albeit an ex-therapist.

Finally at the airport and with some time before my flight, I stopped by a bookstore. I picked up a book about a girl falling from the sky because I liked the cover and I felt a little like that girl. I felt like I was slowly falling and I was a little worried about the landing.

The plane ride home was uneventful, if a little protracted. We had waited on the tarmac for an hour. I talked with a lovely young woman, Claire, on the airplane before we both succumbed to the pull of sleep. She was just about to be married to her high school sweetheart and was moving to Austin to be with her husband-to-be. I kept thinking what a lucky man he is: marrying his sweetheart who was willing to leave her hometown to be with him. When we touched down it was after eleven, and when I finally got home it was after midnight. The cab pulled up to the dark house and I realized there would be no talking tonight. Steph *hadn't* waited up for me. It was too late for the early riser. Our talk would have to wait until the morning. Not the scenario I had hoped for but not surprising. Steph was a morning person.

I walked upstairs, unloaded my bag in the hamper, brushed my teeth, washed my face and climbed into bed next to my sleeping girlfriend. I tried to get close, to feel her body heat, but I rolled away from her unable to accomplish anything. I fell asleep to the sounds of gentle breathing.

* * *

I'm floating in a forest of blue hydrangeas. The leaves and flowers are caressing my skin, tickling me as I go by. In the distance, a shimmering figure emerges. I squint but can't make out who it is. I stop floating and the person reaches out to me, calling out my name. My heart is flooded with joy, my smile widening. I like this place. My nose follows the scent to a nearby flower and I inhale deeply, taking it all in.

"Devan, wake up," the mysterious person whispers. Why would I do that?

"Devan. Please wake up," someone said.

"Do I have to?"

"Devan, I have to talk to you."

I opened my eyes and look around. Steph is sitting at the end of the bed, fully dressed and ready for the day. "What are you doing, Steph?"

"I'm sorry, Devan. I've met..." she paused, looking for the right phrase, "The One. I've packed most of my things."

It was as if Steph had pulled out the plug in my toe letting my joy seep out onto the bed. The joy took with it my comprehension, thought processes and everything else I might need later on to make it through this day. "What?"

"I have some questions on a *few* things. I think I deserve them, but I wanted to ask you first."

"What?" What was she talking about? I sat up and shook my head but it wasn't helping.

"Wake up, Devan, and listen." She stood up and turned on my lamp. "Do you want these things?" She handed me a piece of paper with scribbles on it.

"No, I don't." Steph turned to go. "Where the hell are you going, Steph?" She looked back at me and I saw her eyes. Sad, distant eyes I didn't remember seeing before. How had she gotten this far away from me?

"I'm leaving," she said like it was clearly the only choice she had.

"I know we have problems but do you really have to leave like this?" I asked.

"Yes. I've met someone else."

"Yes, I get it...The One. Why were you even looking for someone else?"

"I wasn't looking, Devan. It just happened. Don't tell me you haven't thought about leaving."

"What the hell are you talking about? I would never leave like this." Thinking and doing are two entirely different creatures.

"I'm sorry, Devan."

"Go to hell, Steph."

She went into the closet and grabbed a box, walked past the bed and went downstairs. I could hear her packing all the things she was taking. Then she left, quietly shutting the door behind her, carefully locking it to keep me safe.

She's met The One?

That pisses me off. I thought *I* was The One, her reason for existence, the only thing that brought joy into her life. She'd told me this so many times it became a joke between us, a tag line on my name. Apparently, the real joke was on me. "Hi, I'm Devan, Steph's patsy." All the things she'd said that made me feel special, all the things she did to show me how much she loved me...were they all lies?

A cat screeched outside, jarring me back to the present, back to my bed where I had curled into a fetal position...alone. I begged the hydrangeas to come back, pleaded with the ceiling to erase the last few minutes. It didn't happen. Coldness crept up from the floor and washed over the cavernous bed. I pulled the sheets tighter around me but I no longer felt safe and comfortable there. "Come on, Devan," I said to myself, "Get up, do something."

I sat up, swung my legs over to the side of the bed, put my feet on the floor and tried to stand. Not *too* wobbly, I thought I could make it to the bathroom. The closet floated by and the emptiness assaulted my senses. All her things were gone. The bathroom rushed up to me and I stood by the sink looking at the holes scattered throughout my things: her toothbrush was gone. Her deodorant was gone. Her hairbrush was gone. She had *really* gone.

I let my legs guide my way downstairs to the kitchen, past the big screen TV we just *had* to buy and our big purple couch we couldn't live without. I inhaled sharply. I couldn't find the coffeemaker. Tell me that bitch didn't take the coffeemaker! Now I was *really* pissed. Granted, Steph bought it, but come on! I dug around in the kitchen, opening drawers and cupboards looking for tea or hot chocolate, anything to soothe my insides. Way in the back, in the cupboard above the spot where the coffeemaker used to live, I found an old container of instant coffee. I heated up the water, mixed the coffee, added sugar and let the bitterness of the brew mix with the bitter taste in my mouth. Not that I was really bitter, mind you. Bitter is such a harsh, nasty little word. I whirled around and threw my coffee mug against the far wall. Steph had just flushed five years away like it meant nothing. I was stunned by her betrayal and by the fact I just smashed my favorite coffee mug. I reached in the cabinet and pulled out Steph's favorite mug, smashing that against the wall. I should probably stop smashing things.

The coffee had been too bitter and thick for my empty stomach, I felt a bit nauseated. I looked back at the sugar and realized I had added salt to my coffee. The wall didn't seem to mind.

I needed something to warm up my cold insides. I leaned against the kitchen sink and I saw my beloved hot tub just outside the back door, seemingly one of the few things Steph had bought and *not* taken with her. Well, not yet anyway. My body was numb but my brain wouldn't stop spinning around and around. I stripped off my pajamas, next to the tub, not caring who saw me naked in the backyard. I climbed into the hot tub, also not caring that I didn't shower first. I didn't care about much of anything at that moment. I hoped the bubbles and jets would drown out the ugly thoughts spinning in my head, but they just weren't strong enough. How had I not prepared myself for this day? I was obviously clueless. I really wished people, okay, Steph, would hold up big cardboard signs, to help me focus: "Do I seem distant and distracted to you? Ask me about my new girlfriend!"

Last night I hadn't even noticed that Steph's things were gone. My mom always said I had selective vision and hearing. I only noticed and heard things I wanted to. Steph had become very distant the last few months, but wasn't that normal for couples after a few years together? I didn't realize Steph would actually leave without talking about anything beforehand. How could she not say anything about her feelings when clearly she had some very strong ones hiding in her tiny heart?

Steph was older than me and always came across as so wise and worldly. She was attractive—her slowly-going-gray, now-dyed jet-black hair wonderfully matched her tanned skin, dark eyes and full lips. Her easy smile and relaxed demeanor immediately put a stranger at ease. She could sell anyone anything, a real estate agent who previously sold Toyotas. We met at the Toyota dealership in Austin, Texas. I walked in with absolutely no intention of buying anything and walked out with a new Prius and a new girlfriend.

Steph later told me she had to knock over three salesmen to be the first one to talk to the "stunning redhead" on the sales floor. Steph knew a lot of people, but because she felt the need to hide her "deep, dark secrets" didn't have any really close friends. At work, she didn't want to be known as the "lesbian salesperson." This allowed her to focus her attention exclusively on me and our relationship. Steph had told me repeatedly she would intertwine our financial lives so tightly I wouldn't be able to get away from her. She joked about how both our names would be on so many documents, I couldn't leave her…it would be too time consuming and difficult. She knew I was way too lazy and cheap to go through the process of hiring a lawyer or an accountant. At the time, I took this to be a deep commitment from her toward our relationship. Clearly, I was wrong.

I had to get out of the hot tub—it was getting a little too hot. Either the heat or the constant barrage of thoughts, or perhaps both, had made me dizzy. I intended to make breakfast, sit on the couch and watch TV. I forgot the food and forgot to turn on the TV. I did manage to get dressed. The couch beckoned me. I lay back on the cushions and slowly pulled myself into as small a ball as I could. I stayed there for a long time, periodically opening my eyes to stare out into the emptiness. I felt a little hopeless. Steph and I had planned everything in accordance with "the rest of our lives." The rest of my life as I know it is now over. The thought that I wasn't good enough for Steph, not good enough for the rest of *her* life, fought to take over my now fragile mind. I didn't want to think about it anymore. I wanted to call a friend, someone who would understand what I was going through, someone who could help me deal with this. But I didn't know anyone like that. Steph saw to that. She slowly closed off my relationships until it was just her and me convincing me that by being openly gay, she couldn't afford to alienate clients who might not be as liberal as we were. If it hadn't been for my brother Brian's insistence we stay in touch, I might have lost him too.

While I lay on the couch time kept moving until the sky grew darker and the shadows longer until they congregated in the middle of the room, eating all the spare light. The ache in my stomach grew until I realized I was hungry—I hadn't eaten all day. I made myself a bowl of pasta, ate a few bites and wandered around the house Steph insisted we buy, a glass of wine in one hand and a hanky in the other, looking for things belonging to Steph, things that might accidentally crash to the floor and shatter. I noticed everything that Steph had bought was gone. Had it been like this for a while? Or did she move things out while I'd been gone for a week?

Where was that weird little man holding the surfboard? Come to think of it, I hadn't seen that for a long time. Had she been slowly moving things to The One's house while I wasn't paying attention? I'm surprised to find we didn't have any pictures of the two of us. I can't remember ever going to have our picture taken. Maybe Mom was right when she said I only saw what I wanted to see. I didn't want to see how bad our relationship had gotten. How distant we both were becoming. How come it's easier to see other people's problems rather than our own? How can I blame Steph for becoming the person she was becoming when it seems I was doing the very same thing?

I walked around the house, finally stopping in the office, looking up at my various degrees and certificates that Steph had proudly insisted I display on the wall. The neat frames pulled my mind back to an earlier time. I was born and raised in Seattle, went to school at the University of Washington and after graduating in psychology stayed in the area to do clinical work.

I worked in my mentor's clinic in Seattle for several years before I realized it wasn't for me. One of the basic questions asked of every psychology major was, "Do you have the patience to work with the same people for years?" I thought I did but had no idea what patience meant. My patients discussed the same problem session after session, seemingly with no real desire or ability to remedy their situation or change anything about their behavior. I had no idea how to help them. Studying the theoretical aspects of psychology had been a joy but actually working with patients had been too much for me. I finally had to step away and reevaluate my life.

When I decided to change careers from a therapist to a teacher, I took my brother Brian up on his offer to stay with him in Austin, Texas. He'd researched the steps needed to become certified as a public school teacher, and it was much easier to do so in Texas than Washington. I reasoned that I could work in Texas as a teacher while I went to school for the required classes for certification in Washington. The chance to get to know my brother better was an added bonus. So a few years ago, I decided to pack my bags and leave the comfort of home for worlds unknown.

Brian is much older than me. When I was growing up, he was already pretty much an adult. Brian moved to Austin years before to be with his wife Nancy, a native Texan. They had a young son, Oliver, and I'd just found out several weeks ago that they were pregnant with child number two. I had moved in with a pleasant guy whom I vaguely remembered from my childhood years and ended up feeling closer to him than I thought would be possible. Brian and Nancy treated me with so much love and respect, not caring in the least when I told them about my love for a woman, that I didn't want to leave when I bought the house with Steph. Or more specifically, when *I* bought the house and was kind enough to let Steph live there.

Steph didn't like to go out much, and she didn't like my brother and his wife. She told me they were trying to sabotage our relationship. She would never explain why she felt that way, but she was wrong. They tried to include her in their lives but Steph wouldn't associate with them at all. Brian and Nancy had eventually developed serious reservations about Steph, feeling that she was too secretive and moody. I tried to explain to them that Steph was raised by wolves, but they just laughed and said you can't really blame the wolves, not decades after your childhood.

I found a wonderful job where I could finally feed my lifelong love of the arts. I had initially intended to return to my home state, but after finishing my Washington certification requirements, I stayed teaching in Texas because Steph didn't see the point in living anywhere else and told me repeatedly she would not leave Austin. So I stayed to be with her. It's funny how the road of life is so bumpy and twisted. I felt abandoned, alone in the great state of Texas where I now felt perhaps I had been long enough. But I had a house and a job I couldn't abandon, didn't want to abandon.

Steph talked me into giving up everything for her, and then she left me holding on to more than I wanted. Did Steph ever really love me or was she just closing the deal on me too? Was a Prius the only thing she wanted to sell me that first day she saw me?

I didn't go back upstairs. When it was time for bed again, I dozed on and off all night on the couch. I didn't have any visitors in my dreams, no more blue hydrangeas to tickle me, no more strangers filling me with profound joy. My heart felt heavy, preventing me from fully breathing in and out.

The next morning I sliced an apple and some cheese, took a couple bites, didn't like the taste, and decided to wrap them up and stick them in the fridge. I would either force myself to eat them or throw them out later. I made s'mores with a side of wine for lunch. I prefer to eat s'mores from a campfire, but a gas stove works in a pinch. I watched all four movies in the *Alien* series, applauding my favorite heroine Ripley, who tried to make me feel better with her toughness and no-nonsense approach to life. I cried and laughed and yelled at the screen. When Sunday evening came around, I told myself I had to get my act together, had to get up in the morning, get ready to interact with people, with my fellow teachers and the kids in my classes. I couldn't break down. I wasn't ready to share that much of myself with people. I wasn't ready to explain Steph to anyone at work, wasn't ready to venture out from the safety of my closet. Not just yet.

* * *

When I couldn't bear the thought of spending another night by myself I decided to call Brian and Nancy. I was hesitant, unsure of Brian's willingness to hear my relationship problems. More specifically my lack of a relationship problem. Nancy chided me about not calling sooner and how quickly could I get to their south Austin home? She told me not to worry as she had wine, tissues and s'mores makings, if that's what I needed.

Nancy answered the door, glass of wine in hand, smile at the ready. "Come in, Devan. Come in." She handed me the glass, gave me a warm hug and peck on the cheek and stepped aside.

"I'm sorry to throw my problems at you but I was driving myself crazy alone at the house."

"Don't worry about a thing. You should have called to talk yesterday, Devan, but Oliver's in bed so talk freely."

In the living room, Brian was holding a hug ready for me. "How are you doing, Devan? Do you need anything to eat? We have some brisket left over from dinner."

"That would be great Brian. Thanks." We moved into the dining room and Nancy pulled out the chair at the end of the table for me and sat next to me. As I ate, I told them the long drawn out version of Steph's leaving and her unexpected and infuriating explanation of finding The One.

"So she left you for The One and then gave you a list of all the things she wanted?" Brian asked from his place on my left.

"Yes."

"The bitch," Nancy exclaimed.

"Amen, sister." It felt great to talk with other people besides myself.

"Are you going to work tomorrow?" Nancy asked as Brian took my dishes into the kitchen.

"Yes, I would rather go to school and be busy with the kids than sit at home and stew in my anger. I just want to put this chapter of my life behind me."

"I don't blame you. What are you going to do about the house? Didn't you put the mortgage in your name only?" Nancy asked.

"I don't know what to do about the house. Yes, I bought it. I paid for the mortgage and Steph paid for all the utilities. Paying for both will be very tight. I shouldn't have paid that much for a house."

"Why don't you get a roommate?"

"I can't see myself doing that. I'm too old for a roommate. I just want to move on. Maybe I'll sell the house."

"Why don't you go on a date?" Brian asked as he came back in with a glass of wine, reclaiming his chair.

"Are you serious? I am not ready to date."

"It's too soon, Brian. She's only been single for two days. Give Devan a break."

"I realize it's soon but from my point of view…is it okay if I speak honestly, Devan?"

"Sure go ahead."

"It just seems like Steph held herself away from you and every other person on the planet and I think it's important you realize not everyone's like that. I think you should go out and at least meet new women. You don't have to have relationships just meet someone and go out for coffee or dinner. And you never know who you might meet. You might meet a loser who you'll never see again or a good friend or The One. You just never know." Brian looked down at his glass and swirled it around. "Do you need some more wine?"

"I think I do," I said.

Brian refilled both our glasses and said, "I heard about this gay matchmaker site called Gayharmony…"

"Wait—what?" Nancy asked, focusing her attention on Brian. "You've been visiting gay hookup sites?"

"No! Paul, at work, has been cracking me up with his stories of guys he meets on there. And it's not a hookup site, it's a dating site."

"Okay, good, you had me worried there for a second."

"Don't be absurd, Brian. I'm not ready for anything remotely similar to dating."

"Okay! Okay. It was just an idea."

"Let Devan heal from this one before you try to throw her to the wolves again, honey."

"Yeah, no more wolves for me."

"What *do* you want, Devan?" Brian asked. Nancy gave him an exasperated look only spouses can give each other.

"No, that's okay, Nancy," I said. "What do I want? I want to be loved. I want a relationship I can parade around the neighborhood. I want to be with a woman who really wants to be with me. I want what you two have. The home you've built for yourselves. I want that kind of love. I want to look at someone and know without a doubt that she really loves me."

Nancy reached over and grabbed my hand. "You'll find that kind of love, Devan. I know you will."

CHAPTER THREE

Steph had waited until near the end of the school year to leave me. I only had a couple of weeks left to work and worry about what I would do about the house and how I would pay for it. The house was big enough for roommates, or I could move out and rent it to someone who could actually afford it. I was having trouble thinking straight. The one thing I knew for sure—I had to start living beneath my means. At the moment, my means were virtually nonexistent.

I have always been frugal in life, especially when it comes to spending and saving money. I took a big hit in salary when I switched from therapy to my teaching job. I did have quite a bit in my savings account but I wasn't thinking about buying a house until I met Steph. She had a vision of the type of house she wanted and had her heart set on the eastside house the first moment she entered it. It was really more than I could afford alone but with both our salaries we would be just fine. Alone, the mortgage and utilities would be a struggle for me.

Steph, along with my bank, convinced me I should be the one to hold the mortgage in my name only. Steph's new real estate career had its ups and downs and her salary was a little too unstable, according to the bank. Steph wanted both our names on the title but I insisted if she wanted her name there she could also put it on the mortgage. So we struck a deal: I would pay for the down payment and mortgage and Steph would pay for the electricity, gas, garbage and other bills associated with homeownership.

I realized I needed to stop eating out, not a good thing since I was a terrible cook. More often than not I found myself standing over the sink, crying while eating dinner because I had forgotten an important ingredient or I just couldn't choke down the food. After scraping the contents of my plate into the garbage, I would hug myself, hanging my head low. I was in trouble.

Life came along and helped me to find my way out of it. On the last day of school, a select group of teachers, myself included, were called into the principal's office and told our positions were no longer funded. We were all shocked but I was relieved. In that moment, I felt my decision was made for me. I didn't feel trapped anymore. Relief flooded over me, carrying away the hurt of being let go by the school. Now I could move back to Washington State, back where I felt the most comfortable, back to the one place I yearned for now that I needed to lick my wounds.

I had grown up in a beautiful area, despite Mother Nature's constant barrage of rain. I spent much of my childhood running around the acres of undisturbed woods behind my grandmother's house in Everett. I never had a chance to finish exploring the area completely before civilization came to town, swallowing up my playground of trees.

I immediately started applying for jobs in western Washington, every job I could find from Bellingham near the Canadian border to Vancouver, Washington, just north of the Columbia River. I preferred to stay near the I-5 corridor, the main freeway in western Washington, but decided I could live anywhere in the western part of the state. I loved teaching at the middle school level and was relieved when I was offered a job at Marbury Middle School in Vancouver, Washington, to teach seventh grade art.

I contacted a real estate broker, who bluntly told me there was no way I could sell the house for anywhere near what I paid for it. Was I willing to take a twenty-five percent loss on the house? No. Was I willing to become a landlord and rent the house out? Yes. So, I became an accidental landlord. The house was conveniently located down the street from the University of Texas where there was always a need for more student housing. There was plenty of room in what had been Steph's dream house for several students. I didn't like the idea of owning a "party house," so I chose a reputable property management company, hoping they would only rent to decent people.

I debated about calling Steph to see if she wanted the Jacuzzi, TV or big purple couch, instead of just selling them at a garage sale, but decided against it at the last minute. If she really wanted those things, she could have snuck them out while I wasn't looking, like all her other possessions. Plus, selling the big things would help pay for the gas out to Washington. It was the *least* she could do, considering.

I packed up my things quickly, leaving the couch for the renters. Nobody seemed to be in the market for ten-foot long purple couches. We had bought most of the furniture specifically for that house and the pieces, especially the couch, fit so well. I spent a couple of weeks saying goodbye to neighbors, colleagues and especially Brian and Nancy. I had enjoyed getting to know him and his family, and was a little upset I wouldn't be around for the arrival of the new baby. I told them I would always hold a special place in my heart for my brother and his wife, and promised to keep in touch through Facebook, Skype and holiday visits. I had every intention of following through. I wasn't going to lose the relationship with my brother we had created over the last few years. I wasn't going to do *that* anymore.

I pulled out of my garage, my Prius stuffed to the gills with my belongings, and sat for a moment silently idling on the curb. I was a little saddened by the thought of leaving Austin, my home of six years. It was the place I had forged a relationship with my brother, the place I had explored my sexuality, the place I had bought my first house. But, along with sadness, I had an entirely different feeling. Anticipation. It started in my stomach, a sense of excitement starting from a little seed and building into something I hadn't felt in quite a while. I pulled away from the house with a smile on my face. Something bigger and better was waiting for me in Washington.

As I drove out of Texas, the longest part of my four-day drive (Texas is a very large state), I thought about where I'd been and where I was going. For every mile I put between Steph and me, I left a little of the anger, resentment and hurt behind. Every morning I felt a little lighter, a little happier, a little more like the girl I remembered from my childhood. I had hope, something I hadn't realized was missing in my life until I left the back door open a crack and it snuck back in.

The last leg of the trip home, the drive through the Gorge, left me speechless. The Columbia River, framed by the Cascades, flowed freely through the niche it had created over geological time. Being surrounded by the towering mountains might make some people feel claustrophobic, but they made me feel like I was at home, lying on the couch, wrapped in a blanket, a steaming cup of hot chocolate at my lips. I had forgotten the beauty of Washington and as many times as possible I pulled over to gaze upon the river and the windsurfers. At my last stop, I watched with awe as the masters "saddled up" and rode the waves as if they owned them. I felt myself carried away, along with the windsurfers, to greater heights than I thought possible. Despite the days on the road and that I was dog tired, I jumped back in the car and sailed the last hundred miles, arriving at my new hometown feeling refreshed and rejuvenated.

* * *

Being a Washingtonian meant a lot to me. I wanted to have a Washington driver's license again, so this new job was just perfect. Portland, Oregon (to the south) and Vancouver, Washington (to the north) are located directly across from each other, separated by the Columbia River which creates most of the Oregon/ Washington border. Seattle had become too expensive and crowded, and Portland was in Oregon. Vancouver seemed like a much smaller town than the one I remembered from my youth, even though it's the fourth largest city in Washington State.

While I looked for my own accommodation, I spent a week or so living with Shelly, a friend from high school, who had moved down to the Vancouver area after graduation. I could have stayed with my parents. My dad would love that, but I just wasn't ready to see my mom yet. I wasn't ready for the awkward conversations and the constant feeling of not being good enough for her.

* * *

Early one morning, while scrolling through Craigslist, I saw an ad for a studio apartment above a detached garage behind a home in the Cascade Park neighborhood in east Vancouver. It sounded perfect and I emailed back immediately. I was dying to see the place and called for an appointment even before the landlady could've had time to look at my application. Within the hour, I pulled up to a cute single-level ranch similar to most other houses in the neighborhood. The street appeared quiet and well maintained with very few parked cars.

There was a kid's bike leaning against the front of the house and a frog yard ornament clinging to a banner which said, "Welcome, Friends." Another one said, "Don't forget to stop and smell the roses," with a ladybug beckoning me over to the flowers. A small woman opened the door before I had a chance to knock and I hurried to put on my very best "I'm a wonderful person" smile.

"Devan? Hi, I'm Corin Steiner." She smiled a tired little smile and looked in the direction of my eyes, but her gaze continued straight through me. She didn't move to shake my hand and I didn't force the issue. She moved back to let me in saying, "Please excuse the mess." Yet there was none—at least not in the living room which flowed into the dining area and back into the open kitchen. The interior was white with a few wall hangings, no kids' toys and no clutter. Anywhere.

"Hi, Corin. I like your yard ornaments. They make me want to move in with you right away," I said, hoping that didn't make me sound too eager. I *was*, but I didn't want to *sound* like it.

"Oh, thank you. I just bought them the other day. I thought the front door needed cheering up. They aren't too much are they?" Corin was a couple inches shorter than me and ten or fifteen pounds heavier. She had blond hair and striking, deep blue eyes I only caught a hint of because she was looking everywhere but into my eyes. She came across as very gentle and kind, timid and unassuming, a person who tried to blend into the background, but really couldn't. She also seemed a little bit on guard, but I figured she was just nervous introducing a new person into her house.

"No! They're great. Made me want to stop and smell your roses," I said. "Thanks for seeing me on such short notice. The apartment sounds perfect for me."

"Good, let's go back and let you take a look at it." Corin went into the kitchen to get the keys, with me following close on her heels. The kitchen was entirely white except for a black coffeemaker on the counter. "Nice coffeemaker: does the state issue those at birth now or does Starbucks give them to you as a coming-of-age gift?" I couldn't help myself, I'd only been back for a week and I'd been dying to crack a coffee or a weather joke.

A pained smile spread across her lips as she said, "No, that's my ex-husband Joe's coffeemaker. I keep meaning to send it to him, but I haven't gotten around to it yet. I don't drink coffee, but I can't bring myself to get rid of it. I'll take it out to the garage and put it with the rest of his stuff." Corin grabbed a light jacket from an assortment of coats hanging neatly by the back door. The jacket was yet another conservative layer of clothing Corin was wearing, which seemed to be a theme in the Northwest: people wore a lot of clothing there. I could understand. I remembered that not much of my skin had seen the light of day when I lived here. I was going to have to reevaluate my Texas wardrobe of sundresses, tank tops and shorts. According to the calendar it was summertime, but I had my doubts.

"The apartment is right back here, Devan. I hope you like it," she said. Corin's house was set back from the street and the apartment was located at the very back of the property, above the garage. A large blue hydrangea was off to the side of the stairs, beautiful in its perfect symmetry, four feet tall by four feet wide, its flowers swaying in the gentle breeze. "Unfortunately, you'll have to park out front and walk back here. There's not enough room for both of our cars on the narrow driveway. We can change that around once I clean out the garage and then we can park the cars there," Corin said.

"That's okay. I don't mind. I really need to walk more." We moved down the path toward the rather large, free-standing garage.

"Hold on a sec, Devan, let me put this coffeemaker away." Corin unlocked a side door and went into the garage. I followed her in, being nosy. The garage was packed floor to ceiling with furniture and boxes. It looked like Corin had moved her entire house out there and started over. Everything was stacked neatly and organized with each box clearly labeled by room.

"Wow, this is a lot of stuff," I said.

"These are all Joe's things," Corin replied as she placed the coffeemaker on a side workbench. "Let's go upstairs."

At the foot of the stairs, which led up the side of the garage to the apartment, was an old wrought iron ornamental gate with an arch covered in a flowering clematis vine. The lock on the gate was large and industrial, and obviously brand new. It looked a little odd next to the much older gate and railing.

"That's a giant lock. Should I be worried, Corin?" I laughed a little as I asked this, but I *was* a little concerned about the size. I didn't see the need for a lock back there, especially a jumbo-sized one.

"No. Matt, my brother, had it left over from a job. It really doesn't fit back here, but the price was right," she replied as she unlocked the gate. "Having someone, a woman really, rent this apartment was my brother's idea. He doesn't like the thought of me and Emily living here by ourselves and he knows I can use the extra money."

"I can understand that. I feel the same way. I don't want to live by myself, and I've never had too much money in my savings account." As a matter of fact, I thought wryly, I hadn't been this poor since before my first babysitting job. I had used up a large portion of my savings going to school in Texas and now moving out to Vancouver.

On the way up the stairs, I inhaled deeply, stopped for a moment to take in the sights around me: the trees, the houses, the big backyard. I smiled because I knew, even before I saw the place, I knew this was where I belonged.

"I hope you like it. Matt worked hard fixing this apartment up, working on it in his spare time, getting it up to code to rent out." She swung the door open, and I walked into my new home. It was a large, open room, as big as an oversized two-car garage, with no interior walls. Walking around the room clockwise, starting with the coat closet just to the left of the entry, I envisioned new furniture in the empty space. I could put my new bed right here between the coat closet and the bathroom.

The bathroom was small but functional, with a shower instead of a tub to make room for the washer/dryer. From there, I walked to the tan built-in wardrobe along the far wall. It was large, taking up most of the wall from floor to ceiling, and well organized. Plenty of room for the corduroy pants and sweaters I needed to buy. Around the corner from the wardrobe were French doors leading out to a small deck overlooking the backyard. The small open kitchen had all the necessities: a tiny dishwasher, stovetop, oven, microwave, an apartment-sized refrigerator and a small sink. The tan, glass-fronted cabinets went all the way up to the ceiling. I would have to buy a step stool to reach the top shelves. A spot for a small dining table and chairs on the remaining wall rounded out the perimeter of the apartment, leaving the center of the room for a couch, various tables and a television.

The apartment had more than enough windows, which would come in handy when the sun finally showed itself. Rather than blinds, the windows had tasteful drapes in muted colors. There were various well-placed lights around the apartment ending with a chandelier over the spot for the table and chairs. Everything was sedate and well thought out. I couldn't have done a better job myself.

"I love it. Especially the kitchen," I said.

"Do you really like it?" She asked this with a look of concern on her face. "I could have Matt change the kitchen cabinets if you want. I'm not sure if I like them or not."

"No, no. I mean it. I love everything you've done here." I reached out to touch her on the shoulder. "I can see myself living here."

"Matt's a contractor and he knows a lot of suppliers and carpenters. He got most of the supplies at work, odds and ends nobody wanted after remodels." Corin absentmindedly rubbed her shoulder where I had touched her, shuddered when a chill caught her and hugged herself. "I ran a preliminary background check on you and everything looks great. We can fill out the rest of the paperwork and you can move in tomorrow, if you'd like." She had a look on her face which told me that if I said no, she would be crestfallen. She seemed almost as eager as *I* was for me to move in.

"I would love to," I said, wanting to hug her, but considering it inappropriate. So I just hugged myself.

"Oh, I'm so happy—one less thing to worry about," Corin said. As she left my new little apartment, I stopped and looked around. I was home. I stretched out my arms and twirled around, just once, to seal the deal. I looked around and took note: once I moved in it would never be this clean again. I locked the door and hurried down to join Corin at the bottom of the stairs. I filled out the paperwork, wrote a check to Corin for the rent and deposit and thanked her again.

"There's no need to thank me, Devan. I'm so relieved you like the place."

"But I will thank you, probably a couple more times. You've put a lot of work into the place and I appreciate everything you've done," I said.

"You're welcome," Corin said, coloring a little. I sensed she wasn't used to praise. "Would you like some tea?"

"I would love a cup of tea." I said as I sat at Corin's kitchen table. We talked about my recent travels. The thought of all my moving intrigued Corin, who had lived in this house all her life.

"My parents moved to Arizona several years ago and left me the house. They love it down in the desert, saying the heat is easier on their old bones," Corin said as she joined me at the table with two cups of warm tea. "The cold and rain has never bothered me much. It seems to suit me."

"It's going to take me a while to get used to the weather here again. I haven't been away all that long, only six or seven years, but I really got used to Austin weather. I'm having a hard time staying warm." I swallowed the last of my tea, and took the cup and saucer over to the sink.

"Would you like another cup? I think the water's still warm enough," Corin asked me.

"No, thanks, I'm going to head out to celebrate. I'll see you tomorrow."

"Yes, I'll see you tomorrow."

CHAPTER FOUR

I was pleasantly surprised with the amount of activity in Vancouver's downtown. I walked past numerous shops and restaurants before deciding on a bar on Main Street crowded with Portland Timber fans watching their favorite soccer team on a winning streak. The aroma of bar food enticed me into ordering a beer, cheeseburger and side salad. The salad was mostly for show but it made me feel better about the cheeseburger and beer. When my food arrived, I allowed myself to be carried away with the crowd, and found myself cheering on a team I didn't realize existed until that very day.

After lunch, and one more beer, I went back to tell Shelly the good news. I was surprised to find she actually seemed a little sad, confiding in me her newfound desire to have a roommate. Would I reconsider my moving?

"It's been so much fun having you around, Devan. I'd forgotten how funny you were." She said this from the couch where we were both sitting, feet propped up on the coffee table, beers at the ready. "Why don't you stay here with me? I can move all my stuff out of the spare bedroom, and you and I could have a great time here."

"I can't, Shell, honestly I love the idea, but I really need to spend some time alone. I had a roommate in Austin and that didn't work out so well."

"Oh, why not?" she asked.

"She left me for another woman." There. I almost actually said I was gay to a friend. For the first time. Out loud. Besides Brian and Nancy, and a couple of men hitting on me, I had never told anyone I was with a woman. I felt a small bit of my burden lift away, from finally *almost* telling the whole truth. There was nothing wrong with going slow and gingerly putting that first foot out of the closet.

Shelly looked over at me and paused for a second. "Well, if you reconsider, you can always move back."

"I'll keep that in mind, my friend," I said. I was thrilled, and more than a little relieved that Shelly didn't react more to my almost declaration. I don't know what I was expecting: disgust, anger, hatred, yelling, screaming. Shelly didn't exhibit any of these things. Maybe coming out would be easier than I had believed. I couldn't really entertain the thought of living with her, though. I needed time on my own, time to get my life in order.

* * *

It took only two trips to move my few meager belongings to my new place. I'd left almost everything behind in Austin, only keeping a carload. The money I made from the yard sale was much easier to transport than the furniture Steph and I bought together. I wanted to leave the heartache associated with our mutual purchases behind too. I would immediately have to look for furniture at thrift stores or end up sleeping and sitting on the floor.

It was on the second trip back when I ran into Corin's daughter Emily. She ran over to check out the stranger who would be living behind her house. Emily looked like a younger version of Corin but with very dark, long hair. Her eyes were exactly the same as Corin's, a deep royal blue.

"Hi, you must be Emily. My name is Devan."

"That's a cool name, Devan, way cooler than Emily," she replied.

"Oh, I don't know about that, I'm very fond of the name Emily. It's one of the classics. I enjoy reading poetry and one of my favorite poets is named Emily...Dickinson. Have you heard of her?"

"Is she the woman who wrote *Withering Heights*? My mom has that book."

"No, Wuthering *Heights* was written by Emily Brontë, different writer, but also very good," I said with a smile and a little laugh.

"I guess there are *lots* of us out there. I don't know of any other Devans, though."

"That's okay. I like to think of myself as unique. I'm sure there are more than a few people out there who are very happy for the fact there's only the one Devan," I said. Emily was cute and she looked a lot like her mother, but more alive and hopeful. "How old are you?"

"I turned eleven in April. I've been alive a whole decade plus one year. How old are you?"

"I've been roaming the earth for just over three and a half decades," I said, feeling a little old next to the eleven-year-old. "Do you have a boyfriend yet?"

"No! My mom says I shouldn't worry about boys until I'm thirty...and married."

"Good advice. Your mom's pretty smart."

"Yeah, she told me once that she wishes she had waited a little while before she got married. She got married really young, I guess."

"Sounds like she knows what she's talking about."

"She also said to marry someone who really loves me, not someone who just pretends to love me. I think she was talking about Dad. He's pretty mean to her sometimes. I even saw him hit her once." Emily had gone very quiet, very still.

"Can you help me unload the rest of my stuff from the car? I could really use the help, Emily."

"Sure. I can do that. Let me just go tell Mom where I'll be, in case she comes looking for me," she said as she ran over to the house. I wished I had her energy. We spent a few minutes unloading the car, Emily leaving a box inside the door and running down to get another one. On the way to retrieve the last box, she was sidetracked with the sudden urge to do cartwheels. She seemed to be having so much fun, laughing and falling over, I decided to join her. I went over, managed to land on my feet and spent the next few moments collecting the change which had been tucked away in my front pocket. Emily thought that was the funniest thing she had ever seen, my change forming an arc around me on the way over, and she lay on the ground, laughing so hard she stopped making any noise.

"Hey, you could help me pick up this change, you know," I said unable to sound mad. "At least start breathing, please." She wasn't able to get up and I finished retrieving the coins before she stopped laughing. "Never mind, I'm done."

"This was fun, Devan," she said while still lying on the ground. At least she'd stopped laughing at me.

"Really? Because if you think this moving stuff is fun, you can come over any time and learn how much fun you can have cleaning a bathroom. Or, better yet, cooking."

"No, not that! That doesn't sound like fun. The laughing part." She was lying on her stomach, her head propped up on her two hands, looking up at me. "I just wish Mom and I would have more fun together. Ever since my dad left, my mom has been sad and upset. We just don't have fun anymore."

"It's hard being a parent, Emily. I don't have any kids of my own, but I can only imagine how hard it would be to be a single mom."

"Yeah, I guess. Is it okay if I come over to your place sometimes and hang out with you?" she asked, a little shyness creeping into her voice.

"Of course you can. Just knock on my door. It's good to get away sometimes, isn't it?"

"Yeah, sometimes when my mom is sad, it makes me sad. I try to be good, but it gets hard after a while. I think she misses my dad, a little bit, but she says she doesn't. She says we're better off without him, but I don't know. I don't get to see Dad very much anymore."

"Well, if your mom is sad and you can't make her feel better, you can come on over and we can play a board game or cards or something, okay? If that's okay with your mom," I said.

"Okay. I should probably go home now." She stood up and brushed the grass off her clothes.

"Tell your mom I said hello, and feel free to come over whenever you need to get away."

Emily helped me upstairs with the last box and said, "Okay, see you later, Devan." I heard her yell, "Hi, Uncle Matt!" on the way down the stairs. I looked out and saw a young man walking toward Emily, pick her up and twirl her around until she half yelled, half laughed for him to stop. From my vantage point, Matt appeared a couple inches taller than me, was well built (*someone* was good and went to the gym), with California surfer boy dirty blond hair, blue-eyed good looks and an infectious smile.

"How's my favorite niece?" Matt asked after he put her down.

"I'm your *only* niece," Emily corrected him, and playfully punched her uncle in the stomach. I decided eavesdropping from my apartment was too difficult, so I made my way down the stairs to meet Emily's uncle. He almost glowed, radiating a carefree aura.

"True, but you're still my favorite," Matt said with a smile. "Why don't you go check on your mom, Em, and let me introduce myself to your new friend. I'll be there in a minute."

"Okay, Matt. Bye, Devan!" Emily said as she ran for the house.

"Hi, I'm Matt Pullman, Corin's brother." Matt offered me his hand. Unlike his sister Corin, he seemed to have no issue with being touched. Being near him was like being on the beach: a warm sun beaming down on you, a gentle breeze cooling you off and a summery salty smell in the air which reminded you of all the good times in life.

"Hi, I'm Devan Scott, the new tenant. Very nice to meet you, Matt. I hear you're responsible for my new abode."

"Yeah, I'm the guilty party. Do you like it?" He didn't wait for a response. "Corin told me about you already and I've been in the house dying to come back here and meet the new person.

I wanted to give you a few minutes to get settled in…but I just couldn't stop myself." He looked a little sheepish. "So you're a teacher at Marbury? Emily will go there next year."

"Yes, I love what you've done with the space and yes, I'll be teaching art. I can't wait to get started." I liked him right from the start. He was so enthusiastic and happy. He had his hands on his hips, leaning in to hear what I had to say like it was the most important thing he'd heard all day. "What are you working on now, Matt?"

"A pretty big project right now. But if I could, I'd lie on the couch all day eating bonbons. Since my knight in shining armor hasn't arrived yet, I have to work," Matt said. I could see him spending half the day lounging around and half the day working out to nullify the effects of the bonbons.

"Oh, good plan. What's the big job?" I asked.

"My main client is a recently divorced woman who wants a totally different look from what her soon-to-be ex-husband wanted." He looked around, leaned in to whisper in my ear, placing the back of his hand against his mouth, "I can't possibly tell you any details, but he cheated on her in a very embarrassing fashion and she's taking him to the cleaners. My budget is open-ended and we are spending with abandon." He leaned back and smiled. "I'm having a ball with this one."

"Ha! Well, spend away. It couldn't hurt, not in this economy."

"I don't mean to be presumptuous. Okay, that's a lie. But would you like to go with me and a couple of my friends to Ladies' Night at The Rainbow Tavern? It's the local gay hangout here in Vancouver. We try to make an appearance once a month, check out the local scene."

"Oh." I was a little surprised. Most people never questioned my sexuality. They just assumed I was straight. After my *almost* declaration to Shelly, maybe it was time to jump fully out of the closet, get a fresh start here before someone kicks my foot back inside and locks the door, trapping me forever. "How did you know I was gay?"

"I have the strongest gaydar in the entire Pacific Northwest." He must have sensed my disbelief because he forged ahead with his explanation. "I don't know if you can tell, but I'm *very* out and proud of *who* I am, and I try to elicit the same feelings in everyone I meet. Plus, it's common knowledge that all women are two beers away from being a lesbian."

"What? That is *not* true! Take that back. Not *everybody* is gay."

"Okay, okay. I was only kidding. You don't have to go to Ladies' Night if you don't want to go."

"No, I'd love to go. What night do you go out?"

"Ladies' Night Out is held every other Sunday, and, it's your lucky day, honey. It's this Sunday. That's normally a school night for you teachers, but it's still summertime and it starts at seven, so you can finish before your bedtime." He said this like it was a funny thing for him. I did just happen to *have* an early bedtime.

"Why are they on a Sunday? What's wrong with a Friday or a Saturday?" I asked.

"Since there aren't any lesbian bars in Vancouver, you gals are at the whim of us gay boys who party a lot more than you nesters. You will *never* find a gay bar willing to give the lesbians one of their Friday or Saturday nights. I guarantee it. But by Sunday, we're pretty worn out by all the dancing and meaningless sex and will hand over the keys to you ladies."

"Oh my, how generous of you," I told him.

"Hey, we have our priorities, honey. Since you seem like such a lovely lesbian, I'll escort you to the party next Sunday," Matt said with a lovely curtsy.

Rallying to match his openness and gaiety, I replied with my own curtsy, "That would be lovely, Matt."

"Here's my number, give me a call later." Matt handed me his business card. "And you should check out the Lesbian Potluck Club here in Vancouver. The boys have had a dinner club for decades and the girls started theirs a few years ago, and I hear it's a lot of fun."

"Thanks, I'll Google them," I said, pocketing his card. "The gay population in Vancouver seems to be very out and about. Not many closets in town." That would take a little while getting used to. Since I have only been with one woman, and Steph wasn't interested in being out and proud, I have never been to a gay bar.

I was too embarrassed to admit this to Matt, but this was a big deal for me.

"Oh, there are a few big closets in town, my dear, but I'm hoping none of them are yours." Matt turned away, gave an exaggerated swishing walk all the way to the back door, and disappeared into the house. He was a walking, talking, adorable stereotype.

Oh, Dorothy, you are *not* in Texas anymore.

CHAPTER FIVE

I called Matt on Sunday afternoon and he gave me directions to The Rainbow Tavern. I showered, put on what little makeup I had and dressed in what I hoped were flattering clothes. I wore a dark gray skirt that ended mid thigh, a crisp white collared shirt I left unbuttoned *just* enough to give a hint of my little black bra, and two-inch heels I prayed wouldn't cause me to fall over. I even shaved my legs, after realizing the "hair through the panty hose" look wasn't a good one. I checked myself in the mirror, hoping for something just above disaster, surprised to find an attractive confident woman ready for the world.

I wasn't really ready for where I was about to go, but I do like to think I am worldly. I'm not, but I want to believe I am. I was so nervous I could barely walk, even without the heels and I had trouble eating dinner. Not a good thing when one is going out to drink and dance. I wasn't sure how I would react to seeing nothing but gay people in a friendly and inviting setting. I just hope I don't stare too much.

I found Matt, the center of attention, entertaining a group of women. He was wearing tennis shoes, jeans and an old flannel shirt, looking the part of a straight escort for a group of women. I would have loved to see him in action, but tonight wouldn't be the night for him. He introduced me to his friends, his favorite ladies, he informed me: Cathy, a boutique owner, blond hair, blue-eyed and stunning, wearing a skirt slit up to here and a blouse open down to there. Marti, a massage therapist and Matt's oldest friend from childhood, dressed just like him. Lori, a freelance journalist and photographer, dressed in jeans and a blouse, small, attractive and friendly. And Sam, a tall, buff police officer, an imposing woman dressed in leather who, after giving me a casual once-over, made me a little nervous. I'm not sure why. I don't think I'm doing anything illegal but you never know.

"You look amazing, Devan, you clean up real well!" Matt said.

"Well, thank you, my dear." I twirled around so he could see the back too. "I try and shower once a week, whether I need it or not."

"I'm glad today was that day, you look great," Lori said with a smile, showing me her perfect white teeth.

We entered The Rainbow Tavern and I had a great view of the bar to the left of us. It covered the entire wall. The top looked like it was made from solid glass and the front was glass blocks backlit by rows of colored lights. The bar was a giant rainbow flag! Close to the front door were tall tables and chairs, now filled almost to capacity. Once past the tables, the dance floor reigned supreme. Loud dance music pulsated throughout the building. Two disco balls hung from the ceiling directly over the dance floor and were rotating with dizzying effect. The floor looked like wood but had a bouncy feel almost like a mini trampoline was under the boards. Along the right side were various doors leading to heaven knows where. Too many to be bathrooms alone. As we came nearer to one of the recently vacated tables, I noticed several of the doors had Private signs on them. I would have to ask Matt about those.

The bar area and dance floor were filled with women of all shapes and sizes, colors and ethnicities, sprinkled with the occasional man. Alcohol, sex and desire mingled with the faint smell of cologne. I was trying to take it all in and keep my mouth from dropping open at the same time. This was an entirely different world for me. Nothing in my past had been similar to what I was seeing and feeling at that very moment. I had never seen so many lesbians in one place. I felt a mixture of excitement, anticipation, fear, freedom, shock, all competing for space in my body. When I was getting ready I hadn't realized how eye-opening it would be for me, and after arriving, I didn't ever want to leave.

After we settled at the table, Cathy and Sam immediately left us—Cathy to look for a dance partner and Sam to mingle. She seemed to know everyone in the room, stopping at various tables to hug person after person. I followed Sam with my eyes, awed by her size and presence.

"Don't be fooled by Sam's looks," Marti yelled, "she is the gentlest person you'll ever meet. Sam comes with us to the bar just to get out of the house."

"She does intimidate me a little," I admitted.

"She's a good one to know, very caring, but if she has to take someone down, she doesn't hesitate," Matt bellowed.

"Don't be one of those people, and you'll be just fine," Lori projected.

"I don't plan on it. I'm generally a good girl," I hollered.

We spent the next few minutes talking over the music, Matt, Marti, and Lori trying to get to know me better in the loud bar. Cathy came and went, drinking one exotic drink after another, all paid for by her legion of admirers. A popular song came on, Matt's eyes widened, and he grabbed Marti, dragging her to the dance floor. As it was just the two of us left, I asked Lori to dance. I had grown tired of yelling over the music and wanted to stretch my aching muscles. Lori moved with the ease of a professionally trained dancer, while I just held on for the ride. I lasted for several songs but finally had to admit defeat, leaving Lori with Marti and Matt, wobbling my way back to the table, where I collapsed onto the chair, thankful it had a back to catch me.

"Hello gorgeous," A warm breath whispered into my ear.

"Oh! Shit!" I yelled. If I'd had more energy, I probably would have jumped a mile. "Hello yourself."

"Sorry, I didn't mean to startle you. I'm Kelly Carpenter, would you like to dance?" she asked.

"Could we just sit here for a minute? I'm more out of shape than I care to admit and a little sore. I'm not used to wearing heels and they are *killing* my legs."

"Sure. I don't think I've seen you around. Are you visiting the area?" Kelly asked. She sat on the stool next to mine, leaning one arm on the table and resting the other on the back of my stool. She was tall and thin, with dark hair and skin, and deep brown eyes. If I had a type, Kelly would be it. She had an assuredness about her that was pleasing and she moved as if she had felt comfortable in her own skin from an early age. Her low, deep voice in my ear soothed and comforted me.

"No, I just moved here from Texas," I managed, hypnotized by her eyes and voice.

"Well, let me be the first to welcome you to Vancouver. I *am* the first, right?" She smiled, leaned in close to me, moved her hand from my chair onto my shoulder and gazed into my eyes.

"Yes, you are the first." I was captivated by Kelly. She was dark and exotic, smooth and good-looking. My stomach did a little flop and I looked away, mostly to steady myself. I put my hands flat on the table in front of me, hoping that would stop the room from spinning. I saw Lori and Marti on the dance floor. Matt had found Cathy and the two were dancing with an energy I found exhausting.

Kelly asked me, "Ready for that dance now?"

"Yes, I am," I said.

Kelly took my hand and guided me toward the dance floor, as I forgot about my tired muscles and sore feet. The music demanded quick movements, but Kelly held me against her strong chest and she danced to her own beat. She was a strong lead—all I had to do was follow. Her smell was intoxicating, a mixture of cologne and new-person smell. I inhaled deeply and held on, looking up into her eyes, lost in her dizzying aura. Her breath found its way to my ear and her lips innocently brushed against my cheek.

The feelings she was stirring unsettled me. It was too much too fast, so I stepped back and introduced Kelly to my new friends.

They had been eyeballing us closely, and converged around us with interest. Then we danced some more until I could barely move, until I could barely see, until I knew I had to go home and put my exhausted body to bed. Kelly laughed when I told her I had to leave, not understanding about my early bedtime.

"Here's my card. I should go too. Call me tomorrow whenever you can," Kelly said. She leaned down to kiss me and I froze up, uttering a little "Oh" when our lips met. She laughed quietly and walked toward the exit. I sat down at our table now filled with my new friends, watching Kelly saying goodbye to her friends, surprised it was almost eleven o'clock. At night. I hadn't been up this late and in clothes other than my jammies in a very long time.

"Thanks, you guys, for a great time. I wish I could stay out later, but I really must go home and sleep," I said, disappointed I was such a wimp. There was a lot of: "Oh, you poor baby" (Matt), "Don't listen to him, great to meet you" (Marti), and "I'm right behind you, Devan" (Sam).

I went around the table, saying goodnight and hugging each one close. I'd had a wonderful time and through my hug wanted to explain to each one how much I enjoyed meeting them. Lori was the last on my hug list, and she said, "Let me walk you to your car."

"How did you end up in Vancouver, Devan?" Lori asked on our way out the door.

"My girlfriend and I broke up, in Austin, Texas, and I realized I didn't have a reason to stay there anymore and decided to move back to Washington." Broke up...she dumped me, whatever.

"So you've been here before?" Lori asked. We'd reached the far end of the parking lot and I pointed my car out to Lori.

"I grew up in Seattle," I said.

"Oh, yeah? Me, too."

"What part?"

"Ballard. What about you, Devan?"

"Federal Way. Not really Seattle, I guess."

"Close enough."

"What brought you down here?" I asked.

"I followed my boyfriend here."

"Oh." I'd just assumed she was gay. So much for *my* gaydar. "What does he do?"

"Apparently, he lures young impressionable girls away from their hometowns and then dumps them the first chance he gets."

"Ouch. That hurts. I'm sorry to hear that." I know firsthand how painful that is.

"That's okay. I'm thankful he brought me down to Vancouver." She folded her arms across her chest and looked up at me. "I wanted to get you alone, Devan, to tell you how much I enjoyed meeting you. I was hoping we could go out for coffee or a drink sometime, just the two of us," Lori said.

"I would like that." Now I was confused. Was she asking me *out* out or just asking me out for coffee? Having everyone aware you are a lesbian was exhausting. She handed me her business card, we said our goodbyes and I watched her drive away. I sat in my car for a few minutes, looking at both business cards. My head was swirling. I had one, possibly two dates. Things were looking up. I liked it in Vancouver.

CHAPTER SIX

After Ladies' Night Out, I reined in my excitement, managing to wait until the next day to call Lori and Kelly. I must admit, I didn't think I was ready to date *anyone*, but I was excited at the thought of dipping my toes in the dating pool. That's all I'd do though, nothing more. I arranged a bicycle ride with Lori for this Thursday, and set up a date with Kelly for the following week as well.

On the morning of the bike date, I woke to a pleasant surprise—a bright, warm, beautiful summer day in Washington, exactly the kind of day that convinced people from all over the country to move to the beautiful Pacific Northwest. Not a good idea—it's only like that fifty to sixty days of the year.

Lori, who had brought an extra bike for me, and I pedaled around Lake Vancouver, enjoying the weather and each other. Sun, clear blue water and happy families grilling hot dogs and hamburgers dotted the shore. It was crowded, but not oppressively so, just full of people who rarely see such beautiful weather.

Lori and I came to a halt, found a place for our blanket and spread it out, wishing we had thought to bring more food than bananas and trail mix. Lori returned from a bathroom break and handed me a deep blue snow cone, gripping a dark red one in her free hand. We devoured them, commenting on the sugar content, but at that moment not really caring what it was. I laughed at Lori's dark red mouth and she laughed at, I can only imagine, my dark blue lips.

"Thanks, Lori, I needed that."

"You're welcome, nothing like a sugar bomb after a long bike ride. Won't impair my driving like a beer would, and it's just as tasty." She laughed and leaned forward, wrapping her arms around her legs. "Are you excited about the first day of school?"

"Yes! Excited and nervous. Tomorrow we have to go in to school and set up our classrooms, so that will make it a little easier, but the first day is always a little nerve-wracking for me."

"You'll be great. I have the utmost confidence in you."

"Well, thank you, Lori, that's very kind." I couldn't get a reading from her, even from deep in her eyes, where I'd spent the last few moments searching. "What about you? What are you working on now? Anything scandalous?"

"No, unfortunately. I'm in between projects right now, but I sent out a feeler or two to a couple of papers, so we'll see what happens in the next few days." She lifted her head up, to get a better angle on my face. "Your eyes are so interesting, Devan. I see the hazel part, but what color is the ring around the outside?"

"I don't know, honestly. Sometimes it looks blue and other times it looks gray. Once I swore it was lavender, but nobody would agree with me."

"Yeah, it looks almost blue today. Beautiful."

"Thanks." After a moment of blushing on my part, I cleared my throat and decided to try dipping my toes in the real lake. "Come on." Lori and I splashed around in the water, soaked up as much Vitamin D as we could, people-watched and talked about my relationship with Steph until real hunger drove us out.

I tried to convince Lori to come over and have dinner with me, but she needed to get home to shower. She said she had plans with a friend for later in the evening.

As we were putting the bikes back on her car, Lori leaned over and kissed me. It was quick and I wasn't expecting it so I didn't react much to it.

"I had a great time, Devan. I hope we can do this again."

"Me too. I look forward to it." I wasn't sure what to say. I wanted another kiss though, so I leaned over and kissed her with my hand firmly behind her head. When I pulled away I badly wanted to look around to make sure no one was paying attention but I fought the urge. I had never kissed Steph in public and felt a little like a rebel at the moment. If the world wasn't careful I just might turn to the dark side. I decided instead to giggle like a little girl and blush all the way to my toes.

"I could cancel dinner with my friend if you want to come over." Lori drew me closer to her and whispered, "You could help me shower."

"No, I don't think that's a good idea," is what I said, although parts of my body were not in agreement.

"No?"

"No. I just got out of a relationship and I shouldn't just jump into another one."

"Right. That's probably a good idea. I don't want to be a rebound from Steph."

"I really want to see you again, Lori."

"Good."

We organized coffee after work for the following week and hugged at my car. I hadn't realized how attracted I was to Lori, thinking we would just be friends. Now I wasn't so sure. The thought of going to Lori's house was more than a little intriguing. I wavered for a minute before deciding that wasn't a good idea. Not at this very moment. On the other hand, I had no doubt how I felt about Kelly. I've never felt an attraction for another person like I felt for Kelly. I wanted to be more than friends and I had to be careful when I was with Kelly. I didn't want to run headlong into another relationship where I would end up hurt at the end. Clearly I couldn't see these things coming but I was bound and determined not to get seriously involved with anyone at this point in my life.

CHAPTER SEVEN

On Friday, because this was only a teacher day, I arrived at Marbury Middle School dressed in jeans, a blouse and sensible shoes, carrying my official "I'm a serious teacher" briefcase, ready for anyone and anything. I'm not sure what I had been worried about. Everyone was friendly, helpful and very supportive. I spent the better part of my very first day setting up my room, talking with the principal and vice principal and introducing myself to the teachers. I was especially drawn to a small, energetic special needs education teacher named Linda Murphy. She seemed the friendliest out of the group of friendly teachers around, going out of her way to explain the inner workings at Marbury and pointing out the rooms she felt were the most important: the bathrooms and teachers' lounge. Linda showed me her room and I gave her a tour of mine.

"I like what you've done in here, Devan. I love all the artwork on the walls."

"So do I, those are mostly my past students' and my work, but some you probably recognize from more famous painters."

"Oh, really? And I thought that Van Gogh self-portrait was actually yours."

"No, luckily, my beard isn't that full," I said.

"Thank God," we both said at the same time, causing us to laugh out loud.

"If you *did* have a beard, though, it would probably be red, just like his."

"True, true," I had to admit. We walked through the halls talking with other teachers until we made our way to the library where we sat in the atrium.

"Hey, have you heard about the lesbian potlucks?" Linda asked me.

Linda was the *second* person to peg me as a lesbian. I'm not sure how this made me feel. I was having mixed emotions. On the one hand I'm thrilled at the thought people are viewing me as exactly who I am. On the other, I feel more than a little vulnerable. I felt almost exposed. Did I have a sign on my back that said, "Lesbian located right here," since I moved to Vancouver? "Linda, just out of curiosity, how did you know I was gay?"

"I guess I just assumed." Linda said and thought about how to answer. "You're not wearing a wedding ring, you seem like an open and loving person and you're comfortable chatting with someone who is obviously gay, me. If you're not, you would've quickly corrected me."

"Oh, I didn't realize you were gay. I don't think I can tell when someone is gay. How am I supposed to know?"

"Well, I'm wearing jeans with a button-down, long-sleeved dress shirt and men's shoes," Linda stated.

"That doesn't mean you're gay, though."

"True. I'm also not wearing any makeup, have never had my nails done and my hair is pretty short." She stood and spun around so I can get a good look.

"Again, that doesn't mean you're gay."

"But chances are pretty good, right?" I'm pretty sure Linda thought I was pulling her leg. She sat back down and leaned into her chair.

"I'm just not very good with this. I don't think I have any gaydar."

"Okay, maybe your gaydar just hasn't been activated yet. What kind of a vibe are you getting from me, Devan?"

"Vibe? Um. I'm not sure. Annoyed, maybe?"

"Getting there. I just think you are making this way harder than it should be. And if you ever really want to know, just ask."

"Really? Just ask?" She must be kidding. "I'm sorry young lady, do you have sex with women or men? I can't see myself asking someone that. Although, it would clear up some questions I have on occasion."

"You could be more subtle than that, but yeah. Save yourself the effort of your questioning everything."

"Well, you're good at this. I *am* gay, and actually, I have heard of the potlucks. When do they happen?"

"Once a month, usually on a Sunday. The next one is day after tomorrow at five p.m. You should come with me, it'll be fun."

"Well…" I hesitated.

"Don't worry, I'm not hitting on you, I'm married. My wife is visiting family out of town and she won't be able to join us."

"Your wife?" Did she just say wife?

"Yes, my wife." Linda looked at me like this was the most natural thing in the world for a woman to say.

"You got married?"

"Yes, three years ago we married in Canada but since it's legal in Washington now, we got married here last month. I guess you could say we're newlyweds!" Linda smiled and showed off her ring.

"That's great! I'm so happy for you." I was happy, I had just never thought about marriage before. I don't know how I feel about the whole institution.

"Thanks. We're pretty happy about it, too."

"But I didn't hesitate because I thought you were hitting on me. It's a potluck, right?" I could feel the color rising to my cheeks.

"Yes. The host provides the meat and the guests provide the sides. Bring whatever you want."

"Well, do I have to cook it? I'm not much of a cook." Actually, I *suck* as a cook.

"Is that what you're worried about?" she said with a laugh. "Don't worry, you can bring anything you want. Something store bought, or chips and dip, or fruit. It wouldn't be a lesbian potluck if it didn't have a bunch of fruits there, right?"

"Oh, thank heavens you have a sense of humor. I'd love to go to the potluck."

* * *

I went back and forth with myself on what to take to the potluck. I finally decided on muffins and cherries, both of which looked too good to pass up at the grocery store. I wasn't sure what the dress code of a potluck was, so I went with my usual standby: skirt, blouse and comfortable flats, in case I had to stand up a lot.

Linda told me the monthly potlucks were held in various members' homes, those with room enough to hold twenty-five or so people. This month's was being hosted by the founding members of the group, Helen and Charlotte, two gracious and friendly women who welcomed me with open arms, hugging me like dear old friends. I was astounded with the friendliness of the lesbians in the community. It had brought me to the verge of tears on a couple of occasions.

I was struggling with all the emotions the move to Vancouver had created. I went from not really having any friends to being surrounded by apparently loving, caring people who didn't care who I slept with, who actually embraced who I would choose to sleep with. It was overwhelming sometimes, when I looked back and saw how very little living I did while I was in Austin.

"Hi, Devan, nice to see you again," Linda said when I made my way back to see her. She was sitting with a diverse group of women. "Join us." Linda introduced me to all her friends, all of whose names I promptly forgot. That's something I'd have to work on. We sat around, drinking wine and getting to know each other. When dinner was ready, we formed a line and dove in, the smells of roasted chicken and potatoes mingling with the sounds of silverware and laughter.

Linda and I sat next to each other outside and talked about the weather and about starting a new school year. We talked with the women sitting next to us and laughed at jokes. The women sitting on either side of us got up to make a dessert run leaving Linda and me alone.

"How's life treating you, Linda?"

"It's a little lonely right now. Ronnie went to visit her cousins in Colorado and took the kids with her so I'm all alone with the animals."

"How many kids do you have?"

"Three. Do you have any kids?"

"No, my ex didn't want any kids. I'm kinda on the fence about having kids."

"Well, kids can be amazing. They're a lot of work too. At least that's what Ronnie says when she's explaining how I never do anything to help her."

"Does Ronnie stay home with them?" I wasn't sure how much I should ask my new friend about her marriage. I should just skim the surface but the therapist in me wanted to dive down deep and explore the bottom of the ocean.

"Yeah, she does and it's stressing her out a little. I'm thinking her stress levels will drop once school starts and she'll just have the one at home."

"Probably. My mom always told me the only thing she wanted to be when she grew up was a wife and mother but that thought made me laugh when I was younger. I think I'm a lot more open to the prospect now."

"I think Ronnie had the same vision when she was younger." A new set of women joined us bookending us at the table.

"What did you bring to eat, Devan?" a woman whose name I forgot asked.

"I brought a variety of muffins and cherries."

"Oh, aren't you funny?" Linda said and everyone laughed, except for me. What was so funny about that?

"Yeah, that's me, the funny one," I said smiling, going with the flow, which made everyone laugh even harder.

I left the potluck full of joy and chicken. The warmth and camaraderie stayed with me, lifting my spirits and offering a sense of so many possibilities and opportunities.

CHAPTER EIGHT

I woke up the next morning excited and nervous on the first day of school, waking up early—probably the only time it would happen all year. I was one of the first to arrive, waiting by the door until the janitor let me in. I was jazzed up on adrenaline, a bagel and coffee, a feeling which would only last until mid-morning at best. Linda arrived shortly after me and we hugged, something I was learning lesbians do a lot, and talked excitedly about the day ahead. Another teacher joined us and Linda casually mentioned her wife, Ronnie, and I stopped breathing, waiting for the other teacher to say something. When that didn't happen, I resumed breathing and relaxed, just a little bit more, into being gay myself.

It could be a sticky situation, being a gay school teacher, especially in Texas, where most weren't very open about it. In Texas, one put up with, "God only knows what THOSE people are teaching our kids…" and other equally ridiculous ideas. The big swath of land from Texas in the middle of the country through Georgia to the east and up into the Carolinas is called the Bible Belt. Texas had always claimed to be the belt buckle of the belt. Texans were the same people who elect school board members who voted to stop teaching evolution and teach creationism. Except for pockets of areas in Austin, Texas was a conservative Bible-thumping state filled with a lot of people who don't care about me or my "freedoms."

It was better in Washington, but I think a few of us still felt comfortable keeping work life and home life separate. Linda was very open about her sexuality, shockingly so it seemed to me, and talked very lovingly about her marriage. I wasn't sure if it was because of her work with special needs kids, or just because she seemed to be the type of person where it never occurred to her to lie about her life.

By the time our lunch break rolled around, my morning buzz had disappeared as predicted and I really needed some food. When Linda looked for me and sat down at my table, I felt like I had been picked first for the softball team. Linda was brimming with activity, her brown hair cut even closer to her head, and wearing a pantsuit that was, if not exactly flattering, very practical. I had a feeling that Linda ran around to keep ahead of the exhaustion that threatened us all. She probably dropped off to sleep the minute she sat down and relaxed, so her answer was never to stop moving. "Are you feeling okay, Devan? You look a little tired."

"Is that code for you look like crap?" I asked. I unwrapped my sandwich, which looked great when I made it that morning, but now looked pretty sad next to whatever was in Linda's Tupperware. I recognized the scent of sausage, tomato sauce and onions, some of my very favorite foods.

"Oh, God, no, you look great. Your shoulders were a little straighter this morning, that's all. Honeymoons don't last very long, now do they?" She said this with a knowing smile.

"No, I've had a great morning. I just feel a little tired and run down. With all the excitement in my life, I haven't been taking care of myself like I should. I've let the lazy part of me take over." I really needed to get back into shape. My jeans were starting to get dangerously tight. I knew I needed to lose weight when trying to fit into my skinny jeans was like trying to stuff ten pounds of crap into a five-pound bag: shit falling out all over the place.

"Your lunch smells so good."

"Ronnie made lasagna last night with garlic bread and a salad. She likes to cook, which is great because I love to eat. She also loves to clean and organize. I am the luckiest woman alive. And no, she doesn't have any single sisters or cousins you can marry."

"I'm not interested in getting married to Ronnie's cousins, or siblings, or neighbors, or anyone at all. My last relationship, with Steph, ended badly for me and I can't even go there right now." That was an understatement. I still felt like I was lying in the middle of the road, watching the bus drive away, trying to figure out how I was going to get the tire marks off my back. Moving and looking for a job kept me busy, but I found myself sometimes, especially at night, wondering why I wasn't good enough. The psychologist in me knew it wasn't anything I did or didn't do, but the insecure woman in me felt like I had failed somehow.

I wondered to myself if I should talk about Lori and Kelly? I didn't want to jinx anything. Oh, what the heck. "Although, I do think I'm feeling up to going out and dating a little. Nothing serious, just a couple of friendly dates." I waved Kelly's and Lori's business cards in the air. I'd been carrying them around since Ladies' Night.

"Really? You're dating *two* women already? Let me see. So much for not being ready," Linda said. She carefully looked over the evidence and deemed them to be authentic. She looked at me with a newly found sense of awe. It could have been amusement, though. It was hard to tell.

"I had a great time when I went to Ladies' Night Out. The woman I'm renting my apartment from, Corin, her brother Matt showed me around and introduced me to his friends. One of whom, Lori, gave me her number. I also met another wonderful woman, Kelly, and I'm very interested in her. This is doing wonders for my ego, which was badly deflated with the Steph debacle."

"Yes, I know Matt and Lori well. I don't really know Corin though, just through Matt, and I only know *of* Kelly."

"I'm beginning to realize how small a community Vancouver is. I'm not used to living in such a tight-knit city where everyone seems to know everybody else. I didn't really know anyone in Austin."

"Just realize your business is not entirely your own here and you'll be just fine."

"I will, Linda, thanks for the warning."

"Well, I'm in awe. You go, girl," Linda said while eating the meal I wished was mine. "Have you called them?"

"I've been biking with Lori already, and I have a date set up with Kelly for Thursday. They're both interesting and attractive, and I'm looking forward to getting to know new people. I didn't realize how much I have missed having at least the opportunity for good friends in my life."

"Well, as far as friends go…I'm available," Linda said with a big smile. She kept eating her lasagna almost as if she knew I'd steal it if she slowed down and stopped paying attention to it.

"Thanks, I'll keep you in mind," I said, mirroring her smile.

"So, you don't want to get married, you just want to have fun and date for a while. Is that what I'm hearing?" I nodded yes. "That sounds like a great idea. Dating two women at once will keep you busy, so you don't have to think about your breakup. I bow to you, Oh Great One."

"I'm not dating two women. We'll see where it goes with Kelly and Lori. I won't date two women at the same time. That's too much work. And don't call me that." Here she was, eating my food and calling me names.

"Why don't you come over for dinner on Friday night? That way, you can meet Ronnie and the kids, and sample some of Ronnie's cooking."

"That would be wonderful," I said, "what should I bring? Muffins? Cherries?"

"Ha, no, don't get Ronnie going. Fridays are pizza nights. Whatever you like to eat or drink with pizza. But if you want to win over Ronnie from the start, I would suggest you bring over a bottle of chardonnay. After a week of dealing with the three kids and me, and running the house, Ronnie always enjoys a tall glass of wine."

"Well, in that case, I'll bring two," I said, "one for Friday and a spare, in case the first isn't enough." Things were definitely looking up. I got my buzz back after eating with Linda. I had now done more things, and had more plans than Steph and I had the last six months we were together.

CHAPTER NINE

It was Date Night with Kelly! My stomach had an entire colony of butterflies gathered inside as I drove over to the little Mexican restaurant. The butterflies were competing for space, making for an uncomfortable drive. There were a surprising number of people waiting to get into the restaurant. I guess a lot of people *did* choose to go out on a Thursday, instead of staying at home with Netflix and wine.

I followed the hostess to a quiet, out-of-the way-table. Kelly was waiting for me, sipping on a clear fizzy drink. When she spotted me, she stood up, gave me a kiss on the cheek and pulled my chair out for me. She looked wonderfully relaxed and happy to see me.

"Hi, Devan. You look great." I'd taken my time getting ready, working to get my makeup and hair just right. I didn't spend much money on clothes, other than what I thought of as my work clothes, but I had a few dresses for special occasions, like a first date.

"Thank you, Kelly, you look good yourself." She did look good, very good. The color of her jacket matched her deep brown eyes. I sat soaking up her aura, and had an urge to run my hands through her dark, carefully-combed hair. She leaned forward and said something quietly, none of which I heard. I leaned forward and touched her hand. "I'm sorry, what?"

"What would you like to eat? Everything I've seen go by the table looks great. The aromas are driving me crazy," Kelly said.

I perused the menu before saying, "I think I'll have the veggie enchiladas. I need to eat more vegetables and I love anything smothered in cheese."

Kelly ordered for the both of us, with a fresh gin and tonic for her and water for me. I didn't want to drink that night. We settled back, and I started the process of getting to know a stranger, the long dance of a conversation spanning many topics.

Kelly was an entrepreneur: starting a small software or IT security business, working hard getting it up and running, then selling it to a much bigger company for a very large profit. She'd done this many times, and was quite good at it, preferring the beginnings of the company, the struggles and problems that arise in the process. Once a company was on stable ground and making money, she no longer had much interest in it, preferring to leave it to her employees to take care of until the right buyer came along. She spent most of her free time looking for the next great idea.

"So, you start a company knowing you'll eventually sell it?" I asked.

"Yeah, I know that probably seems a little weird to you, but the real thrill is to see if I can do it, if I have what it takes to get that specific business up and running," Kelly said.

"Do you ever fail?"

"Sure, a couple of times my companies have failed and those are the best experiences. Before you say anything," she must have seen the look on my face because she laughed, "I learn a lot more from the failures, what not to do, than with the successes. Sometimes a failure is about luck and timing, but other times there's something specific that has gone wrong. Now, if I'd had *several* failures, I wouldn't be so happy about them, but one or two have helped a great deal."

"How many companies have you started?"

"I stopped counting after a few. Maybe ten or so?"

"Wow, it sounds like you're doing very well. Is it off-putting to invest so much money in something that might not work?"

"I don't like to use my own money. I just provide collateral. I borrow the money and only use my own money until the business turns a profit," Kelly said.

"What about emotionally? Is it anxiety-producing to put yourself out there?"

"No, I usually get what I want. When something doesn't work out...usually it does, but when it doesn't, I learn from the experience so it doesn't happen again."

We ate our dinner, talked more about our lives, and about our futures. Since I had eaten such a healthy dinner, we decided we would top it off with a dessert of marionberry cobbler with a side of vanilla ice cream and whipped cream on top. Kelly refused my offer to split the bill, and walked me to my car.

"What are you in the mood for now? Drinks? Movie? Dancing?" Kelly asked, clearly not realizing it was way past my bedtime already.

"I should probably go home." When had I become such an old lady? "I'm sorry. I'm just not used to staying up this late on a Thursday night. I'm usually in bed snoring loudly right about now."

"Oh, sexy!" Kelly said with a laugh. "Nice visual."

"Sorry." It was true though. "Thanks for the wonderful evening." This was my least favorite part of a first date...the ending. Before Steph, when I was dating men I would always rush through the end of the date and give them a nice big hug before they would even think of kissing me. I didn't know if I should kiss Kelly or give her a big friendly hug. I stood next to my car, hoping she would end my turmoil, when she leaned in to kiss me.

It was a warm and sensual kiss, without any other part of our bodies touching, just a melding of our lips. The exploratory kiss ended when Kelly pulled away, gave me an inquisitive look and immediately apologized. "I'm sorry, I should have asked your permission first."

"No, it's fine! I was just standing here hoping you would make the first move. I never know what to do after a first date. Not that I've had a lot of first dates, mind you." Stop rambling. "You could do it again, if you like."

Kelly stepped into this one, gathering me in her arms, kissing me with a passion that took my breath away. My hands slid up her arms to run through her hair, holding her close. We kissed for what seemed like a very long time. I finally pulled away, somewhat to catch my breath, but mostly to regain a sense of composure. I looked around, praying we weren't putting on a show. I couldn't imagine kissing a woman in Texas right out in the open.

"You are an amazing kisser, Ms. Scott, I could kiss you all night."

"It takes two people to make an amazing kiss, Ms. Carpenter." I held her hands, pulling her close. Our server must have spiked my water. I felt a little giddy. I kissed Kelly again, quickly and intensely.

"You really shouldn't tease the animals, Ms. Scott, we have a tendency to get a little wild."

"I'll take that into consideration."

"I'll call you in the morning," Kelly said. She walked toward a new black Chevy Camaro and drove off. Oh my. Good thing I was close to my car. That goodbye left me on unsteady ground. I was shaking from the intensity, having problems finding the key to the Prius when I realized there wasn't a key but a key *fob*. I'd never felt that way after a kiss. I had to take a moment before starting the car. Kelly made me feel things I had never experienced before. A passion intense and unsettling and I kind of liked it.

CHAPTER TEN

On my way over to Linda and Ronnie's I stopped by the store to pick up the wine for Ronnie and dessert for the kids. I figure what kid (of any age) doesn't like a little sweetness to finish off dinner?

Linda greeted me with a relaxed and large smile. We hugged it out and she gave me a tour of their small house, an adorable 1925 bungalow in the Hough neighborhood. The original hardwood floors ran throughout the main living areas with carpet in the bedrooms. A brick-red fireplace surrounded by built-in bookshelves was the centerpiece of the living room. Numerous windows let in plenty of natural light.

The finished basement appeared to be where the kids spent most of their time, their toys neatly put away and organized, a ping-pong table folded up in one corner and a pinball machine in the other. I could have spent a good amount of time down there myself, as I immediately felt at home in the Linda/Ronnie household. It was comfortable and intimate. I have always favored the older style of homes with definitive rooms versus open floor plans. It made the house seem warm and cozy.

The house in Austin was a wonderful example of contemporary living. The house was a dream home with an open floor plan, plenty of room for the professional couple and no bothersome yard to mow. The high-end finishes would make any upwardly mobile person smile with glee. The carefully placed and very expensive furniture great for company to sit and gaze upon the wonder of the house. The only thing the house in Austin needed was a loving family to live there filling up the space with warmth.

Not only did Ronnie and Linda have three children, but two dogs, three cats and a parakeet that guarded the door. The kids were playing a loud, lively game of Sorry! at the kitchen table. Their playing made me nostalgic for the few times my parents played Yahtzee and Monopoly with Brian and me. It didn't happen often, but when we did, I loved it.

When they decided to have kids, it was Ronnie who chose to quit her teaching job and stay at home with them. I'm sure it was a struggle financially to only have one paycheck coming in, but they seemed to be making it work. Linda had told me that Ronnie didn't mind running the household, and she didn't mind working in the yard.

The completely remodeled kitchen was modern and spacious enough to have an eating nook big enough for six—seven or eight if you didn't have an issue with personal space. We ended the tour in the kitchen and Linda introduced their kids: Cameron, eight, the big sister to two younger brothers, Evan, six, and Sebastian, three. The boys were naturally louder and more boisterous than Cameron, who spent most of her time laughing at them and rolling her eyes.

I could feel that little twinge near my heart, the one that started when I lived with my nephew Oliver. The twinge was asking me if this scene was what I needed in my life. I stood back and watched Ronnie and Linda interact with their kids, unsure of my answer. I would loathe giving up my many freedoms, but this kind of love was hard to live without.

"I hope you like pizza, Devan," Ronnie said.

"I love pizza," I said, settling down at the kitchen table. "One of my favorite things."

"Me too!" yelled Cameron, beating her brothers to the punch. "Lots of cheese, please!"

It was a make-your-own pizza night and the kids jumped in headfirst. Cameron took the lead with the two boys watching her every move. When the air had cleared of pepperoni, black olives and mozzarella, I ventured over to try my hand. The kids had finished putting their pizza in the oven and had resumed their game in the time I chose my toppings.

Ronnie had laid out all the toppings you could want on a pizza and some I wouldn't dare put on one. I tried to be good and only have vegetables on mine, but Ronnie had cooked sausage and I couldn't help myself. I added onion, red pepper and, my favorite, black olives to help offset the sinfulness of the processed meat. The kitchen smelled like a pizzeria. The scent of mozzarella mingled with the pepperoni to create a little slice of heaven in the air. I put my finished pizza in the queue and followed Ronnie and Linda through the small hall into the living room where we could easily hear the timer.

"Would you like a beer or some of your wine, Devan?" Ronnie asked before she sat down and got comfortable.

"I would love a beer, thanks, but the wine is for you, Ronnie."

"Thank you, Devan. I think I'll have a glass."

"I feel so guilty, being waited on, AND eating pizza and drinking beer. I really need to work out more, since eating better is something I'm not very good at."

"You should go check out Finesse Fitness on Main Street," Linda said. "It's owned by a friend of ours, Alex, and it's a great little place. She can introduce you to personal trainers and nutritionists. It was touch and go there for a while, with the gym, but Alex is doing great now."

"I think I will. Is it a hardcore gym? I'm not very strong, puny really, and don't want to look too pathetic." It was always a little embarrassing to lift weights next to the big boys in the gym. Sometimes I couldn't find dumbbells light enough to use.

"No, Ronnie and I go there, and pretend to work out on occasion. It's a women's only gym so you don't have to worry about too many big, beefy bodies. Go give it a try, see if you like it. We mostly go to chat and catch up with old friends."

"Be careful of Alex, she'll break your heart." Ronnie came back in with the beer and settled on the couch next to Linda, a glass of wine in her hand. "You'll fall in love with her, madly in love with her, and she'll break your heart. It has happened so many times I've stopped counting. She'll make it seem like it just isn't working out, I don't know how she does it, but it will end. I don't want you to go through the heartbreak."

"Ronnie, honey, Alex doesn't have magical powers. Devan is a big girl who can handle herself."

"I just thought I'd warn you. Sorry, Devan, I don't mean to be in your business."

"That's okay, Ronnie, I appreciate the warning. My last relationship ended recently and I'm not in the mood to have it repeated. I'll put on my best 'chilly' attitude and keep her at arm's length." I was *not* going to go through *that* again. I didn't care if Alex *did* have magical powers.

"Just remember my warning when you meet her. She will charm the pants right off of you if you let her," Ronnie replied.

"Trust me, she won't get my pants off, even if I'm wearing sweats."

"Not up for any toe-curling sex, eh Devan?" Ronnie asked, looking very innocent.

"Ronnie!" Linda was apparently shocked Ronnie would ask me such a thing.

"What? I'm just curious," Ronnie said, looking more innocent.

"I won't be having sex with Alex or anyone else anytime soon, thank you." I replied, the prude in me locking up my chastity belt. "Anyway, I don't see what the big deal is about sex. It's okay, but not that big a deal."

"Oh, honey, you've never had sex then. Linda did this thing once…"

"Oh, saved by the timer!" Linda yelled and jumped up to check on the pizzas. She looked as uncomfortable as I felt. "Just in time, if you ask me," Linda muttered on the way back to the kitchen. I'm glad the oven timer went off, glad it switched our topic. Why were some people so enamored with sex?

Dinner was delicious—nothing better than pizza and beer on a Friday night. After dinner, the kids talked me into playing a game of Sorry! and it was the most fun I'd had in a long time. The family was so easy to be around, so full of love. I let it sweep me away. I forgot about all the world's problems and let out the uninhibited joy of the little kid in me.

While Ronnie and the two older kids were in the kitchen cleaning up the dishes, Linda and I went out into the cool evening to drink a beer on the front porch. Even with the bright lights of the city casting a glow over the night sky, we could still see thousands of stars. The porch was big enough to hold two Adirondack chairs and a bench, which probably held the whole family. I chose an Adirondack chair, as content as I could be at the moment, full of beer and pizza, and happy where life had taken me. Linda asked me to talk more about my relationship with Steph and I told her more than I meant to about the hurt caused by Steph's leaving me for The One, the vague feeling I was just one more deal Steph closed and my desire not to be with someone like Steph again. Our conversation came around to the topic of Alex and Ronnie.

"Please excuse Ronnie. I don't know what's gotten into her lately. She's been saying the most inappropriate things, mostly about sex."

"That's okay. I wasn't offended." I wasn't offended—just a little shocked by her openness about sex.

"And don't listen to Ronnie, okay?" Linda said in a whisper, looking up at the stars. "She dated Alex for a while, many years ago, and Ronnie was very upset when they broke up. I think, all these years later, she still carries a little torch for Alex. She was Ronnie's first and I think the relationship was more important to Ronnie than Alex."

"Sometimes one person is more into the relationship than the other. I won't be getting involved with Alex, so Ronnie doesn't have anything to get upset about. Actually I had a great time on the date with Kelly."

"Oh, yeah? Good for you. I just want you to make up your own mind about Alex. I like her, but I don't see what the fuss is about. She's friendly enough, but I didn't fall under any spells when I met her. I had been with Ronnie for several months before I met Alex, so I could only see *Ronnie* in that way, but I didn't fall over or anything when I met her."

"I can take care of myself. Nothing bad will happen to me unless I let it," I said.

"Good. I like you, my new friend, and I don't want anything bad to happen to you." Linda said and leaned over to pat me on the shoulder. I had to smile. It had been a good night. I wished it didn't have to end.

"Linda could you come help me?" Ronnie asked, opening up the screen door and leaning out. "Sadie just vomited up a giant hairball in the bathroom and it's making me gag."

And…Time to go.

CHAPTER ELEVEN

I woke up Saturday morning feeling pretty good. Making new friends in a new city. I pulled the shades back and looked out the window. Rain. One of our many weather jokes in the Northwest: What do you call the beautiful sunny day which follows two rainy, dark days? Monday. It looked like a good day to hit the gym but I needed a little time to read the paper and drink my fill of coffee first. I had decided the night before that I needed to devote my extra energy to bringing my body back to somewhere in the vicinity of being in shape. I'd let myself go in the last few years, and I was really beginning to look the part.

I couldn't allow myself to dwell on Steph any longer. More than that, I no longer had to follow her schedule or plan my activities around her wants and needs. It wasn't until I'd put two thousand miles between us that I fully realized how much Steph had dominated my life and relationships. I was still relatively young and attractive. And I was happy, even if I didn't have The One following me around. I figured if I worked on my body, really trimmed and toned up, I could be proud of myself. I hadn't been able to make Steph stay with me...but I could make her wish she had. Not that I planned on seeing her ever again but just in case I ran into her at the airport.

When I walked into Finesse Fitness, I knew I'd found the right place. It was the type of gym where I could feel at home: small but with all the necessary equipment, loud and lively but gentle, nonthreatening and inviting at the same time. As I entered the front door, I saw free weights and resistance machines on the left side and the cardio machines on the right. The walls on the weight side were covered floor to ceiling with mirrors to check both one's form and one's hair. There were a few women working out, but it wasn't crowded. The counter was located about five feet into the room and a woman sat hunched against one side looking miserable. This nose-blowing, sickly-looking woman *couldn't* be *Alex*.

"Hi, is Alex around?"

"I'm Alex."

"Oh. Hi, Alex. I'm Devan Scott and Linda Murphy told me about your gym." I walked up and leaned on the counter, taking her in. "Are you okay?"

"Yeah, I'll be okay, just a little sickly today. I'd shake your hand, but I don't want to infect you."

That was an understatement; she looked pretty bad. She wore thick gray sweats and running shoes. Her nose and eyes were red and she was breathing heavily through her mouth. She had a strange puffy look and I couldn't help but feel sorry for her. She sat hunched over with her elbows on her knees, her chin in her hands. I thought about Ronnie's words from last night and smiled at the memory. I would not miraculously fall in love with this woman, let alone touch her. I feel safe from the magical spells of Alex the Great.

"No offense, but you look pretty bad. Thanks for not touching me. Is it okay if I work out today? I know I'm not a member, but could I give your gym a try? You don't have to get up." I leaned back from the counter and gave her my best "Feel better soon, kid" encouraging smile. "I'll find my own way around."

"Sure, have at it."

"You really should go home and sleep it off," I said, trying to be helpful.

"I will as soon as I can find someone to fill in for me. I don't feel good about calling friends this early on a Saturday morning. I have to show up and open the doors. I can't have clients come over and sit outside a locked door. Most people work out early in the morning or late in the evening. I can't afford to lose people because I pissed them off. Once I post my hours on the door, I'm held to those hours."

"I know what you mean. At one point in my life, I was a therapist and when I had to cancel appointments it was a real pain in the ass. People get in their daily routines and don't respond well to change. Sometimes you can't get around it though."

"Yeah. I think working out every day helps with my immune system, but lots of different people touch things here. I have to keep reminding myself not to touch my face. I think that's how I introduce germs into my body." Alex shifted in her seat, leaning forward a little. "You were a therapist? What do you do now?"

"I'm a middle school art teacher. I've always had a passion for art history and painting. After I decided I wasn't a very good therapist, I went back to school and got my teaching certificate and never looked back. I really enjoyed studying psychology, but when I started one on one, I just couldn't do it. My patients would come in, week after week, with the same problems, and it seemed like I just couldn't help them. After a couple of years, I realized I'd made a huge mistake."

"Good call on switching careers. Sometimes the hardest things for us to realize are our limitations, right?" Alex smiled for the first time, a slow smile, breaking through her illness, dazzling in its intensity. "Don't let me stop you. Go work out. If you need anything, I'll be curled up right here on the floor."

"Okay," I said, matching her smile, "and if you need anything, I'll be on the elliptical right over there crying and sweating profusely."

"Ha, good to know. Nice to meet you, Devan."

Alex seemed very easy to talk with, but I definitely wasn't falling for any magical charms. My mothering gene wanted to wrap Alex up in a blankie and bring her a bowl of chicken noodle soup.

I concentrated on my upper body and cardio. I could always come in the next day and work on my lower body or go for a jog. Okay, that was a stretch. I just needed to get through one workout. I looked up and saw Alex staring at me. I waved and she waved back and sat back down. I started on the elliptical, concentrating on my form and the burning in my lungs. The lazy muscles in my legs were twitching like a pinball machine. I moved on to weights, concentrating on the large muscle groups, working them near the point of exhaustion. I finished with my body shaking and trembling.

I managed to make it to the door, waving goodbye to Alex on the way. "Are you leaving so soon, Devan? I could spot you if you need someone." She got up again and tried to come around the counter.

"No, I'm definitely done here. Go sit back down, Alex. What do you mean so soon? I've been here for what—an hour?" I looked at the clock on the wall behind the counter and tried to remember when I'd come in.

"Okay, thanks. I would help you though, if you needed me. And you've only been here for fifteen minutes."

"I have not." It certainly felt like an hour.

"Yeah, you have. Where are you from Devan and how do you know Linda? Do you work at Marbury, if you don't mind me asking."

"I don't mind." I leaned on the counter to keep from sliding to the ground. "I'm originally from Seattle but spent some time in Austin, Texas. Yes, I met Linda at Marbury. What about you? Are you from Vancouver?"

"Nice. No, originally my family is from Maui, but my dad came over to take a job with St. Anthony's Hospital in Portland."

"Maui, how wonderful! You must still have family there, right? I've always wanted to visit Hawaii."

"Yes, my sister and I go back at least once a year. My mom and dad go several times a year. You should definitely go when you have the chance."

"I will. Thanks for letting me work out for free, Alex, but I think I'll go home now and lie on the couch until my heart stops this hammering."

"Thank you for coming in today. You brightened up my otherwise dreadful day. I hope you come back soon. I would love to spot you on the bench press. See what you're made of."

"You might be disappointed, Alex, I haven't worked out in quite some time."

"I promise you won't disappoint me. Take care, Devan."

I wanted to stay longer, to talk a bit more, but I needed to go home and eat the breakfast I had unwisely decided to skip that morning. I could have really used an egg sandwich about then, or a bowl of yogurt and granola. *Something. Anything.*

CHAPTER TWELVE

I would love to say I wasn't sore when I woke up on Sunday, but that would be a lie. I hurt in places I would have sworn didn't have any muscles. How long had it been since I'd really worked out? If I couldn't even remember, it had been way too long. My main goal was to look good in board shorts and a bikini top. I could probably get away with it even now, but it would be helpful to tighten up here and there. After looking out the window at the gloom, I'm not sure *when* I could actually wear a bikini here in the Northwest, but I kept one handy in case the situation ever presented itself. That Sunday was perfect for museums and art galleries. I dragged my sore body around Vancouver's beautiful new main library, a wonder for us book lovers. I loved the space, from the little café downstairs all the way up to the deck upstairs with its lovely view of the empty lot next door. I could put a little trailer on the empty lot and spend my free time next door soaking up the library.

I wandered around downtown, trying hard not to get wet, walking through various shops, looking for things I couldn't live without and unique gifts. Whenever I found something interesting, my practical side reared its ugly head and yelled at me to "put that thing down and get the hell out of here!" After conferring with my practical side, I decided grabbing a cup of coffee was perfectly acceptable.

Coffee shops were a wonderful place to be around people but spend time doing solitary things such as drinking a wonderfully warm cup of coffee and catching up on the latest news via the local newspaper.

I drove home with little traffic, marveling, again, at where life had taken me. I still couldn't believe that I'd really moved back home, back to where I could *breathe*. I parked out front and walked around to my little place in the back. I was so wrapped up in my thoughts I didn't see the very intense, angry-looking man standing by the gate. The very gate which led up to my apartment.

"Oh, I'm sorry, I didn't see you there. I hope I didn't frighten you," I said, because he was frightening *me*. I hadn't seen him at all coming around the corner. He was hard to see in the dwindling light as he was dressed in black from his hair on down to his shoes. He was a little taller than me, maybe five-eight or five-nine, but seemed as wide as he was tall, and built like a tank. He oozed anger. I could see it rolling off his head like steam from a hot football player on a freezing night.

"Who are you? What are you doing back here?" His arms were crossed over his chest and he was eyeing me with more than just curiosity. I don't believe he really cared who I was or what I wanted.

"I'm Devan. I live here. Who are you?" I was more than a little concerned being back there with him alone. I tried to form a game plan, but didn't feel threatened to the point of yelling and screaming, or at least not just yet.

"I'm Joe Steiner, and this is my house," he said. His words were quiet but they were spat out with anger.

"Okay. Is there something you need?" I was growing more concerned. The part of me which yearned to yell and scream seemed to be making sense.

"I need some things from the garage, but my key doesn't work." He looked at me for a couple of seconds, turned on his heels, and walked off into the night. I swear he said, "Fuckin' bitch," as he walked past me, but I couldn't be sure.

That was creepy. My inner voice told me he was *not* a good man and that I should call the police, but I decided against it. He hadn't actually done anything to me. If you could have someone arrested for being mean and ugly, there wouldn't be too many people left to walk around free. I walked over and knocked on Corin's back door. I had to let her know that Joe was walking around her backyard. The house was quiet and still. I knocked again and the drapes parted a fraction of an inch, and Corin opened the door.

"Hi, Devan, so nice to see you, please come in."

"Hi, Corin. Sorry to bother you."

"No bother, always glad to see a happy face." Corin gave me a little smile and motioned for me to sit at the small kitchen table. "Is everything okay? Do you need anything?"

"Everything's great, for the most part. I just need to talk with you about Joe." I wanted to see her reaction and it was not surprising. She tensed up, lost the smile and looked a little nervous. She turned her head a little and looked behind her like she was afraid he was sneaking up on her.

"What about him?"

"I came home tonight and almost walked right into him. I have to admit Corin, he's a little scary."

"Yes, he can be very scary." She looked into my eyes. "Are you okay?"

"I'm fine, Corin, I'm just concerned about *you*. He was in *your* backyard doing heaven knows what. Does he always prowl around like that?"

"I don't think so. He's been staying away, since I filed the restraining order."

"Restraining order?" Now I was worried. I leaned over to touch her arm, but she pulled back like I was going to burn her. She looked embarrassed and moved to grab my hand when I waved her off. I needed to remember she didn't like to be touched. She motioned for me to sit at the table. "Did he hurt you?"

"He hit me, once. He said I provoked him, but I didn't mean to."

"Has he always been abusive?"

"No. Joe and I married when I turned seventeen. I was so much in love, and my parents loved him too. He was thoughtful and caring, suave and older. He swept me off my feet, which wasn't hard to do. He told me how much he loved me, told me he wanted a lot of children, painted a picture I so desperately wanted to be a part of." Corin had that look in her eye, the look of love and loss, the pain of having to grow up too fast.

"Did he change after he married you?" I asked. I'd heard this story so many times before.

"After a while. At first, he was very loving and supportive. He worked all the time, traveling a lot, but when he was home, he was very affectionate. He didn't start to change until I became pregnant with Emily. He seemed to lose interest in me, telling me he didn't want to hurt the baby." She looked up from her hands, startled she hadn't been the perfect host. "Can I get you something to drink?"

"No, I'm fine. What happened then?" I knew I shouldn't pry, but this was interesting. I found myself relaxing back in the chair, my voice soothing, wishing I had a pad and pencil to take notes.

"When Emily was born, he carried her around everywhere, calling her '*meines kleines Madchen*' or his little girl. He wanted to have more kids, but I'd had complications with Emily and I couldn't have any more. He totally lost interest in me then and focused his attention on Emily." Corin clenched her hands together and looked down at the table. "Joe and I started to fight and he became very mean. He told me he didn't want to have sex because having a child had aged me. I was always young looking for my age and he liked that fact. He didn't want to sleep with an old lady."

"How old were you?" I asked.

"About twenty. I told him to leave me if he didn't want me and he said that would *never* happen. Something about the way he said it terrified me. I talked with Sam, a police officer friend of Matt's, and she said to get the hell out, she would protect me, but I couldn't. I didn't think he would let Emily go that easily. He really adores her."

I reasoned that Sam was probably the same woman I had met at Ladies' Night Out, the slightly intimidating one that everyone assured me was a pussycat deep down. "What finally made you decide to leave him?"

"About a year ago, he got mad over something I had asked him and hit me. Pretty badly. Emily saw it all and she was very upset. I was recuperating in the hospital, when Sam and Matt talked me into leaving him. I couldn't run, though—this house has been in my family for years. Joe went to prison for a while, for assault, but he managed to get out after six months. Exemplary behavior, they said. Sam keeps trying to convince me to move out of state, but I just can't seem to bring myself to leave this house. It's all I've ever known."

"What do you think he was doing in the backyard?" I had only seen him standing there. He could have been doing anything before I walked up.

"Well, all his things are back there. Maybe he needed some clothes. I had all the locks changed after he left. Sam insisted I at least do that."

"Maybe you should call the police. He's in violation of the restraining order, at the very least," I said, at a loss for what else to do.

"You're right. I should call the police." Corin got up to get the phone.

"Maybe Sam will be the one to come over." I said because it seems Corin has a fondness for Sam.

"Sam's been my guardian angel." Corin smiled and had a faraway look in her eyes. "She still comes most nights to see how I'm doing. I don't think I could have left him if I didn't have her looking out for me."

She called the police and an officer, not Sam but Officer Burkov, came by to take our statements. He said they would issue an arrest warrant for Joe. He had violated the restraining order to stay away from Corin.

"Thank you, Officer Burkov, for coming over to help," Corin said.

"You're welcome, ma'am. Take care and give us a call if you need us." Officer Burkov left us alone in the house, telling us to keep our doors and windows locked. He said he would try and swing by when he wasn't busy but he couldn't promise he would.

"I feel better now." I said.

"So do I. Thanks for letting me know Joe was here. Do you think the police will find him?"

"I hope so."

Corin's hands got busy moving the placemat into the perfect spot. I took this as my cue to leave.

"Call me if you need anything, okay?" I said. I stood up, wanting to give her a hug to let her know I cared, but not wanting to unnerve her further.

"I'm sorry to drag you into this mess, Devan. It didn't occur to me he would be so bold. I thought him hitting me was an isolated incident."

"Don't worry about me. He looked at me a little weird, but it seemed to be because I made him lose control over the situation and not that he wanted to hurt me." I tried to convince myself it was true.

She moved away from the table slightly. "He's never hurt anyone else, besides me. He adores Emily and her friends. There just seems to be something about *me* he doesn't like." She looked into my eyes, seeming to believe what she said. I smiled, a pained little smile, and agreed with her. After a moment's hesitation, she linked her arm with mine, walking with me to the back door, sending me off to my own life, sealing hers in with the click of the dead bolt.

I ran to the gate, quickly unlocked it, slammed it shut and ran up to the apartment. I checked my little home for any evil men lurking in the shadows, saw the place was empty and tried to relax. I'd just focus on the great day I'd had before Joe crashed into my life. I had almost succeeded, getting ready for bed while humming, brushing my teeth with vigor, but I kept coming back to his face, his fierce, dark, squinty little eyes burrowing into mine. The intensity of the situation lingered, making it difficult to fall asleep. When I did, I dreamt of an evil troll chasing me.

CHAPTER THIRTEEN

Over the years I've tried to be an early to bed, early to rise person, but I've never been able to make it work. I usually go to bed early and wake up late. I can *easily* sleep ten hours a night. That Monday morning it was even harder for me to wake up than usual. I crawled out of bed and hit the shower. As I washed my hair I thought about my introduction to Joe, shivering at the memories both real and dream-like.

I arrived at school in a good mood, not a great one, but one that would suffice. My kids helped, their good spirits filling me with a sense of purpose, a sense of "this is what life's all about." I met Linda for lunch, a new ritual I looked forward to every day, eager to talk about the weekend.

"I met the most disturbing man last night, Linda. Do you know Corin's ex? Joe? He seemed to materialize out of nowhere."

"Stay away from Steiner, if you can. He is *not* a good person." Her cheeriness dissipated and she leaned forward. "Go talk with Corin about him. I think she should tell you herself." That was all she would say.

"That's all I get? Is he a mass murderer? I already talked with Corin and now I'm talking with you. Come on, give me something to work with, Linda." I tried to look exasperated but was having a hard time. My facial expressions never took orders from me. My face pretty much did whatever it wanted to without any conscious input on my part.

"It's not my story to tell. Instead of hearing rumors and innuendo you should just go to the source for your information." Well, wasn't *she* the wise adult at the table? The wise adult who was in the process of unwrapping a sandwich which made my stomach do a little flop and stand at attention. Get ready, stomach, I'm going to disappoint you again.

"But I truly enjoy rumors and innuendo." I paused, waiting for a little tidbit. "No? Okay, I also wanted to say I had a great time on Friday. Thanks for inviting me over," I said, trying not to drool, her food making me sway. "Ronnie and the kids are so much fun to be around. But tell her I'm not interested in Alex. I went by the gym on Saturday and I loved it, but Alex is not my type."

"I'm sure Ronnie would love to hear all about it." Linda finished unwrapping her meatloaf sandwich and laid it down on her plate. "It was a little weird at first hanging out with Alex, but now I can honestly call her a good friend of mine." I had moved from the far side of the table, to sit closer to Linda, to look at her sandwich. "Before you have a stroke, would you like a bite?"

"Yes, please!" Ronnie could really cook the mess out of meatloaf. Oh my, it was good. "How long did they date? What happened to cause them to break up?" I asked and quickly added, "Not that I'm interested, just curious."

"It only lasted a few months but they were very much in love, according to Ronnie. I haven't asked Alex about it. How do you start *that* conversation? But Ronnie said it ended because they wanted different things out of life. Ronnie is all about family and commitment. Alex loves the chase and the honeymoon phase. When that's over, Alex looks for a way out. Not in a horrible, predatory way. Alex just doesn't seem to be the type who can stay in a relationship. Like I said before, this is just Ronnie's side of the story and it ended well. We're all fine with the way things are now, so no blood, no foul."

"I'm glad everything has worked out for you. Dating Alex is the *last* thing I need right now. And if I was dating Alex I couldn't swoon over Kelly now could I?"

"We didn't get much of a chance to talk about Kelly the other night. Have you seen her since then?"

"No, she's busy working on a project in San Francisco and I won't see her until she gets back. I'm hoping that will be the end of this week sometime."

"Sounds like life is good for you right now."

"Yes. I'm having a great time." The proximity of the meatloaf was making me a little delirious. And Ronnie was thoughtful enough to put it on wheat bread, not the unhealthy squishy white bread *I* would have chosen. My bite had melted in my mouth. But I was trying to eat better. I'd brought a salad for lunch, a huge stretch for me since I wasn't a big fan of lettuce. Lettuce was just a serving bed for the steak, cucumber, cheese, black olives, bell pepper, hardboiled egg, Goldfish, cottage cheese and Italian dressing. If I happen to snag a piece of lettuce while eating the tasty stuff, my body considered that a bonus. I could either do a great job working out or eat in a relatively healthy way, but generally not at the same time. If I could coordinate the two activities, I could perhaps do some serious damage.

CHAPTER FOURTEEN

After work I made it to the gym around four p.m. Another great thing about teaching as compared to being a therapist was getting off early enough to beat most of the traffic. Finesse was packed with women, so I needed to time my workout very carefully. Several women surrounded the counter, laughing and talking loudly. This scene was both unexpected and unwanted, as I had hoped to talk with Alex for a minute or two about signing up. The crowd dispersed when I walked in, and there was Alex.

Whoever that creature was that talked with me on Saturday, it was not the Alex I saw before me two days later. *This* Alex had short, dark thick hair and light blue eyes, almost gray, which laughed and seemed to take in everything at once. She had a natural tan and a healthy radiance, an exotic beauty about her. It all shocked me a little considering how bad she looked on Saturday morning. She wore shorts and a tank top, showing off arms and shoulders defined by countless hours in the gym. She was about my height, and looked long and lean. No extra padding on *her*. I bet there was a six-pack under that tank top. She was, by far, the fittest person I had ever seen who was not on television.

When I was finished admiring her arms, I looked up into her eyes. For a second everything slowed down and she was all I could see, everything else in the room melted away. I couldn't help but smile. I looked down from her eyes to her full lips and they curved into a smile seemingly just for me. She waved and broke the spell. I had the strongest urge to make a run for it but I managed to stay and drag my feet in her direction. I felt disoriented and confused, unable to form complete sentences.

"Hey, Devan, what are you up to?"

"Um, I thought I would lift a little today," I said to a spot a little to the left of her head.

"After you're done, come find me and we will talk about signing you up, okay?"

"Sure," I said, pulling myself away and wandering off.

What was *wrong* with me? I see one woman with an amazing body and I fall apart? I will admit it was a very enticing body, one I was not expecting. She must have crawled home from death's doorstep. Most people who join a gym are trying to get into better shape. Very few of us were actually in great shape. I could barely focus on my workout, trying to keep an eye out for Alex, marveling on how many hours she must have worked out to look like she did.

"Are you feeling all right, Devan?" Alex asked, having come up behind me at the weight stand.

"Oh, crap! You startled me. Yes, I'm fine, just thinking about stuff," I replied in that smooth and debonair way I have.

"I was thinking, since there's a lull in the crowd at the front desk, why don't you come over and fill out the paperwork?" Alex turned to walk toward the counter. I couldn't help my eyes from wandering down her body and I wasn't disappointed. Seriously, I thought to myself, what was *wrong* with me? I'm running around like a teenage boy trying to hide my hard-on. There had to be something in the water. Life was never like this in Texas.

"Are you sure you're feeling okay? I'd feel really guilty if you were coming down with my cold. I would feel so bad I would probably have to nurse you back to health." Nurse me back to health? Is that Alex's idea of flirting with me? I wouldn't be totally against it, though. She's probably just being a helpful business owner.

"No, I'm feeling just fine. I don't know what's wrong with me." I shook my head to clear it a little. "You look great today, Alex. I didn't think you were going to survive."

"Some friends watched the gym for me over the weekend so I could rest. I'm feeling much better now. I just slept right through it. I woke up this morning feeling a ton better."

"Well, good for you. Show me where to sign and I'll be heading out to dinner. I'm so hungry I could eat bugs with a side of worms." She handed me the paperwork and came around to my side of the counter.

"Have you been to the restaurant around the corner? It's owned by the friends who watched the gym for me, retired basketball players, and the food is delicious and fresh. They grow their own vegetables on-site but I think they leave the bugs and worms out in the garden. You could probably get them on the side, if you really wanted. I was heading that way myself, care to join me?"

"I would love to." Damn. Think first, then speak. She distracted me with the bugs and worms.

"Great. Let me go tell Ashley we're leaving." She turned to walk away and I had to look again. Wow, again.

"Okay, I'll just be right here signing paperwork," I said, and added, very quietly, "And trying to get rid of this hard-on."

CHAPTER FIFTEEN

"I thought you said this was around the corner?" I didn't want to sound like a wimp, just needed to clarify. When Alex said it was around the corner, she didn't specify *which* corner. We walked, but it was not what I would call close.

Alex smiled, her eyes filling with glee. "What do you mean? This is practically next door."

"I'm going to have to pay closer attention to you," I said, struggling to keep up with the superfit woman striding next to me. "Although, I've had a few warnings about you, so maybe not too close."

"Really? From whom?" Alex stopped and turned to look at me.

"Just a friend of mine." I had stopped too and was a little too close for comfort. I could feel the heat from her body. Her gaze tried to reach in and secure the information, but I was having none of that. I moved along. "I can see it! Here we are. Come on, Alex."

If there is a heaven, I'm convinced it would smell like that restaurant: garlic and onions sautéed in olive oil. I was weak with hunger, barely managing to make my way to the door Alex held open for me and stay on my feet. Crawling to the table would have looked a little silly. There was a line of people waiting, but it seemed as if Alex knew everyone and we were seated immediately.

After walking back to the table, Alex introduced me to the owners of Le Restaurant, Jodie and Michelle. They were very friendly and polar opposites in looks. Jodie was very tall and thin, dark and exotic looking. Michelle was shorter and heavier, blond and fair-skinned. While the three friends were chatting, I had a chance to look around. It was an older colonial house which had been converted many years ago into a restaurant. Strategically placed tables for two were inserted into several nooks and crannies. Our table was located in the very back of the place overlooking most of the immaculate garden, a very intimate setting which was seemingly unavoidable.

"You three seem very close," I said after Michelle and Jodie had left us alone. "How long have you known them?"

"I dated Jodie briefly, a few years back. We still care about each other and Michelle is a great person."

Interesting. Maybe what Ronnie had said earlier had a ring of truth to it?

The waitress came by, hugged Alex and took our orders. I liked the way Alex asked me what I wanted, and ordered for me.

"Have you dated every lesbian in Vancouver?" I asked.

"No, of course not. Don't be silly. There are a couple of virgins out there, waiting for me." She smiled. Oh, she was a cute one. "So, who was warning you against me?"

"A friend of mine was saying I would fall madly in love with you and my heart would be broken because you are incapable of being in a real relationship," I answered.

"What? Who is this so-called friend? That's not true at all."

"It's okay. I'm not looking for a relationship right now, so I don't really care." Our waitress brought our drinks and I took a long sip from my margarita rocks. "Just out of curiosity, what's the longest relationship you've had?"

"Well, let me think." She sat back and thought about it. Long and hard. "Two years—give or take. What about you?"

"I was with Steph for five years before we parted ways."

"Parted ways? That sounds very friendly."

"Um, not very. I just didn't want to say she left me for another woman." I found my drink fascinating at the moment.

"She left you for another woman? She must be crazy." Alex flinched a little and said, "I'm sorry. You used to be a therapist. I won't use the crazy word again."

"It's okay. I don't really mind the way you used it." It actually made me happy. "I always thought lesbians met a woman, moved in and never left. How is it you've never been in a long-term relationship? Do you not want to be in a relationship?"

"Of course I want to be in a relationship. I just don't want to waste my time or anyone else's time. There's nothing wrong with that. I'm waiting for the right woman to come along and sweep me off my feet." Alex seemed to be getting a little defensive. She scrunched up her eyes and gave me a look that I can only interpret as, back off lady! I'll pull back and let my brand-new friend breathe a little. Not everyone likes therapy.

"Are you still friends with Steph?" Alex asked after a few long silent moments.

"No, I don't think we'll ever be friends."

"I'm sorry that happened. It sounds painful for you." She reached over and briefly touched my hand, sending chills up my arm.

"It's okay. She clearly wasn't The One and I'm not sure *how* I feel about her." Oddly, I'd been too busy to analyze the situation fully, which is what I usually do. "I thought I loved her, but I don't seem to think about her that much lately. It hurt when she left, but I find I'm enjoying my freedom, and not having to answer to anyone for anything."

"So you were just together for…what? The sex?" she asked.

"Trust me—we weren't together for the sex. Most days I would rather eat a piece of chocolate cake than have sex."

"You've never really had good sex then, I can tell you. Even bad sex is better than chocolate cake," Alex the sex expert said.

"Sex isn't the most important thing in a relationship, Alex. What about trust, love, respect? There are many things more important than sex." I didn't understand what the fuss was about. Yes, it could be fun and enjoyable, but it could also be stressful and awkward. I've only slept with two men and Steph so my pool of experience is just a wading pool.

"Of course, there's more to relationships than sex. But sex has to be an important part of any serious relationship. If you're living with a person and you don't have sex, you have a roommate, not a relationship. I don't care how long you've been together, sex has to be a part of your life or you're just friends. Yes, sex fades. No one can keep up with 'new relationship' sex indefinitely. I mean, who has the time to stay in bed for the weekend indulging in and exploring every inch of your new love? That would be wonderful, but it does tone down after a while."

Sex for the whole weekend? Who does that? "Enough of the sex talk. You're making me very jittery."

"Oh, yeah?" Alex wiggled her eyebrows. I hate that.

"Not in a good way, Casanova."

Our dinner arrived and we settled in with a much safer discussion. I learned Alex had a twin, Cleo, and they had shared a room growing up until they both decided enough was enough and went to different universities. It was hard on them at first, but in the end it strengthened their relationship. Cleo attended Notre Dame for her bachelor's and master's degrees in accounting and Alex received her degree in exercise physiology from the University of Florida. Their mom was a native Hawaiian who met their dad when he was stationed at Tripler Medical Center in Honolulu. They spent the first few years of their lives in Hawaii but had their formative years in the Portland area, eventually both migrating to Vancouver. Cleo had two little girls, Hailey and Alexis, with her husband, Tony.

"Hailey is named after Tony's sister who died in her teens and Alexis is named after, well, me. Since my family isn't very religious, I'm the children's Guidance Parent. I'll take care of them if anything happens to both their parents. Poor kids." Alex laughed and pushed her plate away from her. She leaned back and crossed her hands in front of her full stomach. "What about you? What's your story?"

"Well, let's see. I have one much older brother, Brian, so I felt like an only child growing up. I went to school to become a therapist, something I had wanted since I was a very young child. I wanted to help people deal with the problems they couldn't deal with alone. I realized, much later, that life isn't that simple." I finished my meal and ordered another drink. "One day I realized I didn't have the skills to be a therapist and went back to school to become a teacher. Best decision I've ever made."

"You kind of skimmed over your childhood there a little bit." Alex said.

"There's not much to tell. I had a normal childhood, no trauma or drama, nothing much really. My parents were tired by the time I came around. As long as I was quiet and flew under the radar, I was pretty much on my own." I stared at my drink, wondering why the loneliness was still there. "I think I became a therapist to heal myself. When that didn't have the desired effect, I decided to teach."

"Do you want kids of your own or are you living vicariously through other parents?" Alex asked.

"Some days I really want a child and other days I realize we have enough kids in the world. What about you? Do you want some for yourself?"

"I love my nieces, but I couldn't imagine doing that myself. Not after all the stories Tony and Cleo have told me. The thought of being responsible for another human being is a little unsettling." Alex looked around the restaurant and turned back to me with a small smile. "Where did everyone go?"

We were the only two people left in the area. Where did the time go? It seems everyone had left and taken the time with them. Alex insisted on paying and my thin wallet rejoiced. We found ourselves outside in the cool air, walking back to the gym. As we drew close to the gym, Alex placed her hand gently on the small of my back, not far enough down to be suggestive, but far enough to be the center of my attention. It felt natural and intimate, sensual in a way that didn't make me uncomfortable. We walked like that, side by side, Alex steering me to my car.

"Thanks for dinner. You really didn't have to pay, though," I said.

"I had a great time—it was my pleasure. You can get the next one, okay?" She leaned in from the side and hugged me with one arm, a feel-good buddy hug. I put my arm around her and hugged her firm body back.

"See you soon?" She looked into my eyes and smiled. She walked over to her car, a deep blue BMW convertible. Nice.

CHAPTER SIXTEEN

It was cold and wet the afternoon Lori and I met for coffee at the Nutt House, a local bookstore/community center owned by the Nutt family. So instead of my usual skirt and blouse, I opted for my new turtleneck sweater, corduroys and boots. I found Lori lost among the books, and we settled into two easy chairs in a corner. People with laptops and various devices were spread at tables throughout the café.

"You look a little cold, Devan. How are you adjusting to the weather?" Lori asked, sitting looking warm and snug in her jeans and T-shirt.

"Aren't you cold? You're not even wearing long sleeves." How could this little person stay so warm? "I'm freezing. Some days I can't get warm enough."

"Don't worry, your body will acclimate after a while. Looks like the Texas weather spoiled you a little."

"I don't remember it being this cold. No wonder coffee has never caught on in Texas like it has here." I looked around the café and into the bookstore, rejoicing once more in being back home. The smell of fresh coffee brewing mingled with the smell of the pastries, and took me back to my college days and the joy of being a part of humanity.

Lori asked, "What part of Seattle are you from again?" Not my favorite thing to do, the talking about myself part, but a necessary way to get to know someone. Lori was friendly and open, caring and thoughtful. Her job as a photojournalist entailed frequent travel and she shared some of her favorite stories with me. I tried to keep *her* side of the conversation going, finding her stories much more interesting than mine. Besides, I'd heard all mine several times before.

"Any luck with work?" I asked.

"Yep. I'm flying out, later in the week, to Broadway to work on an article for *The Advocate* about a Proposition Eight play making its debut. I'll do some background on Prop Eight and review the play, talk about how it is received."

"Sounds interesting. Do you often write about gay issues?"

"Yeah, I like to remind myself of who I am and what's important to me. I also write about women's and environmental issues."

"I Googled you and read some of your articles. You're a great writer."

"Thanks. I'm working on a book too, set in Austin, Texas actually."

"Really? What about?" I was both surprised and thrilled she would write a book set in Austin.

"I don't want to say right now, don't want to jinx it, but a friend several months ago happened to mention something about a series of incidents which happened in Austin and it piqued my interest. I've been slowly working on it for a while, whenever I can. I really need to spend some time in Austin to do some in-depth research."

"Is this your first book?"

Lori responded, "Yeah, the story started out as an article, but got too big. After a while, I realized it might be kind of fun to write a fictionalized story based on the event. We'll see how it goes."

"Well, if you do go back to Austin, and you need help with that research, let me know. I might be able to give you a head start on some of the local knowledge, and I would love to go back and see my brother and his family."

"It's a deal. I'm sure you miss the Tex-Mex, too."

"Oh, my, it's like you can see inside my head," I said with a laugh.

"Nice try, Devan, trying to make it sound like you'd go back to Texas just to see your family and not just for the food." She finished her coffee and went to get us a refill.

We spent the rest of our time walking through the narrow aisles, sharing our favorite books, and laughing at the ones we'd tried to read but could never finish. I confessed my inability to finish *Moby Dick*, try and try as I might. She confessed her strong dislike of Hemingway, not understanding his minimalist style. We both loved *Walden*, wishing we could throw it all away and live in the woods. Not going to happen, of course, but a lovely thought nonetheless.

"I like you, Devan. I can see us becoming great friends." She stopped, put *Walden* back on the shelf, and turned to look at me. She put her hands on my shoulders and leaned in to kiss me. It was short and intense. As she pulled back her eyes asked for more. I leaned in to her and kissed her back.

"Well, maybe not just friends, Devan."

"Maybe not," I said a little lost in my head. Lori keeps surprising me with the intensity of my feelings for her. I wasn't sure what I was supposed to be feeling. I had strong feelings for Kelly and now Lori also. I didn't feel right dating them both but the thought of not seeing one wasn't the right answer either.

"Are you okay, Devan?"

"Yes! I have conversations with myself a lot more than I should, sorry."

"Not a problem. I should probably leave you two alone then." She smiled and made a move to leave.

"No. You don't have to leave."

"I should. I have a few things to do before I leave for work."

Lori walked me to my car, kissed me on the cheek and promised to call when she got back to town. She left me next to my Prius, warm in heart and body. I went home and with the help of strong herbal tea, settled down a little. I was thrilled at the thought of everyone I had met in Vancouver. I now had people to talk to, shoulders to cry on. That was something I missed in Austin. It was funny…now that I'd found people to support me, I didn't feel the need to cry anymore.

CHAPTER SEVENTEEN

After getting back from San Francisco Kelly called, and we set up a date for the coming Friday night. When she asked me if I had a dining preference, I told her about Le Restaurant. She chose to dine at eight p.m., explaining to me why that was a good time to start eating dinner. She clearly didn't realize teachers wake up early and need a good night's sleep. Kelly survived on only four or five hours of sleep.

I arrived a little early, too early to be seated without Kelly. Jodie apologized for not having a place for me to sit and wait. "Alex is in the back, having dinner alone. She has an empty chair at her table, why don't you join her? I'm sure she won't mind." Jodie assured me she would come and retrieve me when Kelly arrived. Why not? Sitting would allow me to kick off my heels and relax. *Why* I felt the need to wear heels, and not something more sensible, was beyond me. They *did* make my calves look good though.

I wound my way toward the back and came around the corner to find Alex talking with a young waitress. Alex had her arm casually thrown over the back of her chair. She was reclining slightly, looking up at the waitress, smiling and talking. I waited, to give them a minute to finish, which gave me the opportunity to watch Alex. She made her workout clothes look good. I walked up to Alex's table, happy her smile expanded when she saw me.

Alex asked, "Hey you. What are you up to tonight?"

"I'm waiting for my date to arrive. Jodie thought I might like to sit down and I think I looked a little wobbly in these heels after a few seconds, and she felt sorry for me. Is it okay if I sit with you for a minute?"

"Yes, please, join me." Alex jumped up and pulled my chair out for me. How very kind. "A date, huh? You don't waste any time, do you? Got right back up on that horse. Who is the lucky girl?"

"Thank you," I said as I sat down, waiting for Alex to sit before I answered. "A woman named Kelly I met at The Rainbow Tavern the other night."

"You went to Ladies' Night Out? I haven't been in a while. How was it? The women must have been swarming all over you."

"There weren't women swarming," I said to Alex's serious face. "Her name is Kelly and I really like her. She seems very friendly. Everyone out here seems very friendly." I couldn't recall meeting anyone in Vancouver I *didn't* like. "I like you people."

"Good for you," Alex replied. Her food arrived and she sat with her hands folded on her lap, not wanting to eat in front of me. I insisted she eat, telling her I would help her eat from the far side of her plate.

"I'm surprised to see you alone, Alex. No date tonight?"

"No. My girlfriend Stacy and I broke up a couple of months ago and I decided I needed to spend some time alone. I'm picking the wrong women. Perfectly amazing women, just not the ones for me."

"Hey, that might be a really great idea, see what's going on with Alex. You know what they say, once you stop looking for love, that's when you'll find it," I said.

"What about you, Devan, do you think Kelly could be The One?"

"Oh, I don't know, it's way too soon. Steph told me repeatedly I was the love of her life and then she *left* me for the real one, so I'm not really keen on the idea of giving someone control over my emotions again. I just want to go out and have a little fun right now. If it works out, then I'll be very happy. If not, I won't be too upset. I won't be falling in love anytime soon."

"Well good. Have some fun. Just be careful." Alex leaned over and put her hand over mine. "You're a good person and I don't want to see you get hurt." Why does everyone think I'll be getting hurt? Or is she trying to tell me something? I need to stop thinking.

"Thanks, Alex, I'll be careful." Her hand was warm and soft, her fingers long and thin. She kept her hand over mine for a second or two and then withdrew, pulling her hands back into her lap. The waitress stopped by and took my drink order, and brought Alex a fresh one. Alex and I spent the next few minutes talking about the weather and our mutual desire for a sunny, warm day.

"Cleo and I are going to Maui for our annual pilgrimage to see family in a few weeks. I'll send you pictures, if that helps."

"No, that would make it worse. Please no, 'the weather's here, wish you were beautiful' postcards, okay? Maui sounds like a wonderful place. You said you flew to Maui often, right?"

"Cleo and I have flown back together every fall since we were able to fly alone. It's something I look forward to and we've only missed a couple of years."

"That's so wonderful. How long do you normally stay?" I asked trying to hold back the little green-eyed monster.

"It depends on the year. We used to go for a couple of weeks, but recently we've had to go for shorter trips. This year we're only going for a few days."

"Why?" Not to be nosy or anything.

"Lots of reasons: Cleo's kids, my work, Cleo's work. Life is getting in the way. It's my desire to buy a little shack out there to retire. I like to dream big."

"Hey, Devan, sorry to interrupt but your date's here," Jodie said after materializing at the table. "Come on." Jodie placed her hand on Alex's shoulder, giving her a smile.

"Thanks for the chair, Alex. I'll see you at the gym." I got up and smoothed out my skirt.

"I'll be there. Take care of yourself Devan."

CHAPTER EIGHTEEN

"Hi, Kelly."

"Hello, beautiful." She got up and kissed me on the mouth. In front of everyone. Yikes, that's a little *too* out of the closet for me.

"Hey, let's sit," I said, hoping to take the spotlight off us.

"I thought you'd never show up. Where were you?"

"I was sitting with a friend, Alex. She owns Finesse Fitness." I took my napkin and laid it on my lap. "Do you know her?"

"Yes, I go there to work out when I'm in town." Our waiter took our drink and food orders and left us alone. "How friendly are you with her?"

"Um…not that friendly. I just know her from the gym," I said. That's a weird question.

"Stay away from her. She'll use you," Kelly said, not looking at me, sipping her gin and tonic.

"Why does everyone keep saying that? I like her. She's funny and interesting. I think she could be a good friend." I reached down for my gin, took a sip, and realized it wasn't my favorite drink.

"Let me rephrase…be careful around Alex. She has quite the reputation in Vancouver." She reached across the table and took my hand in hers. "But I really don't want to talk about Alex. I want to talk about you."

"What would you like to talk about?"

"I want to talk about what you do for fun."

"Well, let's see. I've been thinking about this. I like to go to movies, concerts and plays, those types of things. I like to ride bikes and go hiking. I don't like to go to the gym, not really, but I enjoy how it makes me feel and how it makes me look." As I said this, I thought about how much time Alex spent in the gym and forgot about the rest of my list. "What do you do for fun?"

"I like to run, lift weights, read, travel and go for drives down the coast."

"Oh, I like to take long drives too!"

Kelly responded, "We should take a drive together one of these days. I could show you a few new things." She smiled in an electric way which made the hairs on my arms stand up.

"I'd love to." I would really like that.

Then Kelly asked, "What *don't* you like?"

"Oh, I don't think we have enough time." I said, checking my watch, causing Kelly to laugh. "I don't like mushrooms of any kind, porn…it really embarrasses me, true country music, bad drivers, cooking, lettuce, people who leave their shopping carts out in the middle of the parking lot, littering, children going hungry, and indifference, to name just a few." Don't get me started.

"Okay, that's a good list…or should I say a bad one?"

"Right! Ha! What don't *you* like?"

"Lazy people, timid people, smart cars, cauliflower, museums, cantaloupe, runny eggs, junk mail, almonds and dark chocolate," she replied very seriously.

"Really? Lazy people? Are you sure?" She doesn't know me at *all*.

"Yes, they drive me crazy."

I warned Kelly, "Just so you know, I am a very lazy person."

"No, you're not."

"Yes, I am."

"No, I can tell just by looking at you, you are *not* lazy."

"Looks can be deceiving, Kelly."

"Well, I don't believe you. Nobody who is lazy has a body like yours." As she said this, she gave me a once-over. I wonder if she realized she'd licked her lips.

"Thank you," I said, feeling a little uncomfortable. I'd never had anyone look at me the way Kelly did. I didn't want her to stop. It would just take a little time to get used to her.

"No, thank *you*," she said and smiled. My chicken and Kelly's frittata arrived and we inhaled the aromas deeply and dug in. We talked about our list, clarifying our choices and laughed out loud. How can you *not* like dark chocolate? It goes perfectly on top of a plump, sweet strawberry. I asked her about her dislike of timid and lazy people, as I'm always disturbed when someone looks down on others who don't live up to their standards.

On the way out to our cars, Kelly reached for my hand. "Do you want to go out to the garden and look around?"

"Okay, it's a little dark out here. You'll protect me from the zombies and vampires, right?" Not that I was afraid of the dark or anything. "That doesn't make me timid, does it?"

"No, it doesn't and yes, I'll slay all your demons."

We wandered down the path, marveling at the plants, wondering what they were, holding hands. When we got to the back fence, unseen from the restaurant, Kelly turned to face me, planted her hands on my hips and slowly backed me up against the fence.

"What are you doing?"

"I want you," Kelly said and I saw it in her eyes. I saw her passion, her desire, her want. She kissed me, hard. My desire boiled up from the tips of my toes, rising up through my core and cascading out to my fingers. She ran her hands down to my butt and massaged me. My hands traveled up and I ran them through her hair. She squeezed me so hard, I wound my hands into her hair, afraid if I let go, I would collapse.

Kelly put her leg between mine, moving them apart. She let go of my ass and with her right arm, put her hand between my legs. I matched her movement, with my left, grabbing her hand with mine, stopping her from touching me.

"Wait, I don't think I'm ready," was all I could think to say. Her face, a couple of inches from mine, glowed with passion.

"I want you. Please, Devan." I didn't see any real reason to say no so I let go. Kelly pulled down my panties and she entered me. She leaned down to get a better angle and I placed my hands on her strong shoulders. She thrust with her fingers and rubbed me with her thumb until I came suddenly, unexpectedly and yelled out. I collapsed, thankful Kelly kept me upright against the fence. I couldn't form any words, my breathing labored, and my heart pounding from the excitement of the situation.

"Hello?" Someone called out into the darkness.

"Shit," Kelly whispered, pulling up my panties and smoothing out my skirt.

"Yes?" I stumbled a bit as I walked back into the light, with Kelly at my side. It was Michelle, over by the side entrance to the garden, looking a little concerned.

"Oh. Hi, Devan." She looked toward Kelly, hesitated a moment, and looked back at me. "Are you okay?"

"Yes, I'm fine," I croaked, cleared my throat and kept going. "I tripped over by the fence and it startled me."

"Are you sure?" She seemed not totally convinced by my story. "You look a little weird."

"Yes, I'm fine," I said with a smile.

"I've got her. She's okay now," Kelly said, putting her arm around me, pulling me close.

"Okay then. Be careful back here please." She turned to go.

"Thanks, Michelle. We will be."

Kelly and I stood there for a minute, shaking our heads, and Kelly laughed. "You sure did yell out. I'm glad the whole restaurant didn't run back to shine a spotlight on us."

"Stop laughing." I was not as amused as Kelly was. What if Michelle had come back to the fence a few minutes earlier? I shuddered to think of the embarrassment. "I couldn't help it. You caught me *way* off guard. Next time give me some warning will you?" I started walking toward the parking lot, Kelly hot on my heels.

"You didn't enjoy that?"

"Yes. I did enjoy that," I said. I *had* enjoyed that. Mostly. It was wild and crazy and explosive. How could I *not* have enjoyed that? I did enjoy that, right?

"Can I take you home?"

"I think I've had enough excitement for one night," I replied.

"Okay. I'll call you tomorrow."

"You do that."

She spun me around, kissed me and left me by the side of my car. It was a slow painful drive back to my place. I wasn't used to this much emotion rushing through me. It was a little overwhelming. Never had I been taken like that before and I never knew that was possible. My body felt different, like I wasn't completely in control, like the Devan I know had stepped away, and a newly released Devan had taken over. I kind of liked the new Devan.

CHAPTER NINETEEN

I woke up feeling something resembling desire. Good thing I had coffee and bagels to keep my hands and body entertained while my mind wandered. Seeing the desire in Kelly's eyes was unnerving and exciting. I thought about Steph. It took me a while to get up the courage to sleep with her. Some might say a long while. But throughout our five years, I never felt truly comfortable with her. I wouldn't walk around naked and always kicked her out of the bathroom. Steph was the seducer and always in control, so there was no snuggling and baby talk after sex, we just rolled over and fell asleep. Steph and I planned our days around what each of us had to do individually, not what we wanted to do together. We *did* go out together in public and had fun, but it was usually related to work and I was always her "friend." I'm sure everyone knew we were together we just pretended we weren't. We never went to bars or anything as obvious as a Pride Parade. Steph wouldn't hear of that. We had no gay or lesbian friends. Maybe accepting that it was okay had something to do with the way I was raised.

My mom, Estelle Scott, was a homemaker (because that's what women did back when my parents got married) and my father, David Scott, the man with two first names he used to say, was a dentist who spent long hours at his practice before he retired. My parents were older than what's considered normal. My mother was forty-five and my father almost fifty when they had me, ancient for parents at the time. After having my brother, my parents thought they couldn't have any more children, so when I came along they were "pleasantly surprised." Brian would play with me, on occasion, but I grew up alone. My brother went off to college before I really made an impression on him. My family never showed much affection toward each other, never hugged, never said "I love you." We were all very *cordial* to each other, just not demonstrative. I guess we all just assumed we knew we loved each other, no point actually saying it.

I was a somewhat restless child, unsettled, looking for answers to unknown questions, hoping to stumble upon the arrow that would show me the way. I'm sure I *was* a pleasant surprise for my parents, but they were *weary* by the time I showed up. They had raised a son and had established deep roots in our neighborhood. They had already done Boy Scouts and guitar lessons and various things, showing little interest in what I wanted to do. I spent a lot of time by myself, growing up, using my imagination to entertain me, and trying to keep one step ahead of loneliness. I read everything I could, wrote journals, drew and created new private worlds.

Maybe that's why I wasn't as upset about Steph leaving as I thought I would be. Compared to other couples I knew Steph and I weren't very demonstrative either. Maybe I realized, deep down, Steph wasn't The One for me. We didn't hold hands and we didn't show much affection toward each other, even in private. I don't recall even telling Steph I loved her, come to think of it. I used to think this was the norm. This was how relationships were supposed to work. I didn't think true love was in the cards for everyone. Most of us just find someone who doesn't piss us off too much.

That was the remarkable thing about my feelings for Kelly, especially after our date. I felt so intrigued by her and I barely knew her. I was a little unsettled by the unexpected sex but I could see myself loving her, sharing my life with her. She awakened feelings, long dormant feelings in my body I didn't clearly understand. I very much wanted to understand those feelings though. I was terrified and thrilled at the same time and hated to admit what I was feeling because I didn't want to lose control of my emotions to someone else. It might not work out but I wanted to give it a try. She stirred too much in me to not pursue her.

Kelly called while I was thinking about her, a good omen, and my thoughts and emotions flooded out to her.

"Hi, Devan. How are you this morning?"

"I'm well, thank you."

"What are you doing?"

"I'm sitting here thinking about you."

"Good things I hope."

"Mostly."

"Mostly? Care to elaborate?" I could hear her smile had left.

"Don't get me wrong, I enjoyed myself last night, but I'm overwhelmed by my feelings right now. I've never experienced anything like what happened by the fence. I wasn't sure I was ready and I'm still not sure."

"But you said yes, Devan. I thought you wanted me."

"I wanted what you wanted, Kelly." I had a disturbing thought. "Would you have stopped if I said no?"

"Of course I would have! What do you take me for, Devan?" She made a noise and I thought she hung up but I could hear her breathing.

"I'm sorry, Kelly. I didn't think before I spoke."

"It's okay. I didn't mean to hurt you. I wanted you so badly I couldn't help myself. You are beautiful, Devan."

"Thank you. I've never had someone want me like that. It scared and excited me at the same time. You're beautiful too, in case you're wondering."

"Thank you. Just know you can always say no. I care about you too much to rush into anything you're not ready for. How about we step back and slow down a little? I don't want to lose you, Devan."

"Okay. Do you want to meet for dinner again?"

"I would love that."

She suggested a new Vietnamese restaurant on the other side of town. We hung up and I tried to go back to my coffee and paper. In my heart I believed her. She seemed sincerely interested in my well-being and I knew she desired me. I was grateful for the slowdown and very much wanted to see how our relationship looked on our next date.

CHAPTER TWENTY

On Sunday, I woke up feeling wonderful. My talk with Kelly had settled my stomach and I was ready for the world. I arrived at Finesse around nine—after the serious gym rats but before the late risers—finding it almost empty. I walked up to the counter and grinned at Alex like an eight-year-old just stumbling into a candy store for the first time.

"Hi, Alex. What are you up to this fine day?"

"Um…not much," Alex said. Well, I wasn't expecting fireworks and a marching band but I was hoping for a smile.

"Is this a bad time for you? I could take my good mood home and come back later," I said.

"No. I'm just having a rough morning. What can I do for you?" Alex said, a little more formally than I'd anticipated.

"Nothing. I wondered if you'd like to work out with me. I could spot you first." I swear I was being charming and friendly but apparently I was the only one who realized this.

"I'm not in the working out mood at the moment, Devan. Go work out and have fun. Pam, the woman on the elliptical, always needs a spotter." She turned to yell at the woman. "Pam? I found a spotter for you."

Okay, not the reception I was expecting. It hurt a little—Alex was getting rid of me, pawning me off on a woman I didn't know. I would show her. I could spot Pam like nobody's business. After working out with my new best friend, I walked back over to Alex to tell her how I felt. The more I thought about it, the more it annoyed me. Before I could get a word out, I noticed Alex was on the phone. And crying. Oh, crap, there went my righteous anger. Maybe life wasn't all about me after all.

"Are you okay, Alex?" I asked, after she hung up and had a moment.

"No, I'm not," Alex managed to say. "That was Tony. Cleo was in a car accident last night and was airlifted to Vancouver Memorial Hospital. It's weird, I've had a feeling something was wrong but I couldn't figure out what. When I went to bed last night, I tossed and turned all night. I thought it was about you. She's in the OR right now."

"Alex! I'm so sorry. Come here." I enveloped her in an enormous hug and held her warm body until she stopped crying and pulled away.

"Let's get to the hospital," Alex said.

"Do we need to call someone to look after the gym?"

"No. Let's just go. I'll leave a note about a family emergency. Everyone will understand." As Alex and I were the only ones left in the gym, we closed quickly and jumped into my car. I drove because I was clearly in better shape than Alex at the moment. "What happened?"

"I'm not really sure. I don't think I heard the whole story—thought I was going to pass out there for a minute. Cleo was driving home from the store and someone ran her off the road and down into a ditch. She rolled over a couple of times and they had to cut her out of her SUV."

We found the family huddled in one of the waiting rooms near the OR. There were so many of them, they filled the small room and spilled out into the hall. When we got close, an older gentleman stepped away from the rest and looked at us.

"Alex! There you are. Where have you been? We tried calling you all night!"

"Oh, Dad, my cell phone had died but I didn't realize it until this morning." She sounded like a small terrified child, unable to comprehend what was going on around her.

"I should have come over and gotten you, but I was afraid if I left..." he said, struggling with the words and the thought of losing Cleo. "She's still in surgery." Alex buried herself in his arms and I stepped back away from the sorrow.

I thought of leaving and going back home. I felt a little odd, being with Alex and her family during such an intensely private moment.

Alex pulled away from the embrace, walked into the small waiting room, the crowd absorbing her along the way, leaving me alone with her father. He had the same light blue, beautiful eyes and dark, short hair.

"I'm so sorry about all of this, sir. I don't know what to say."

"I don't know what to say either. I'm Frank, Alex and Cleo's father," he said, giving me his hand.

"I'm Devan, a friend of Alex's. Please excuse me for intruding. I thought I should drive Alex here, make sure she arrived safely."

"Thank you, the last thing we need is for Alex to get in a wreck too." He lost control then and I patted his arm until he settled a little. I'd never hugged my father the way Alex had hugged hers. I didn't know if I could. "Let me go find my wife. I'm worried about her." He looked a little embarrassed having just cried in front of a stranger, a woman no less. "Thank you, Devan." He turned away and followed Alex's path, disappearing into the waiting room.

Then it was time to go. I left a message for Alex with a relative telling her to call if she needed me and how terribly sorry I was about Cleo. I ached for Alex knowing how upset she must be and wanted to be there for her, like any good friend would be. But I didn't feel we were such good friends yet. I felt I would just be in the way so I went home to my little apartment and I waited there for Alex to get in touch with me.

CHAPTER TWENTY-ONE

I was restless and uneasy the rest of the day. I called Le Restaurant and talked with Jodie about Alex and what to do about the gym. She told me she would take care of it and call Alex. I kept busy with cleaning my little sanctuary and doing some schoolwork. I wanted to call Alex to see if she needed anything but I knew she would be with family. I told myself if she didn't call by tonight, I would call the hospital and ask for her.

I heard Corin out in the backyard calling for Emily and poked my head out the window.

"Hi, Corin. Do you need help?"

"Just looking for Emily. She's not up with you is she?"

"No, not today. Have you checked the bushes on the east side of the house? She likes to hide in there sometimes." I decided to join her outside instead of yelling at her through the window. I walked down the steps and joined her in the backyard. "Is she in trouble?"

"No, no trouble. I just like to know where she is and what she's doing. That sounds bad doesn't it?" She almost laughed but instead pulled her sweater around her a little bit tighter. "Ever since you told me about seeing Joe, I've been a little on edge. I don't think he'd hurt Emily but I didn't think he would ever hurt me either so…"

"No, I understand. You're just worried about her." I would be too. Corin went around the corner just as Matt and Marti rounded the other corner.

"Well, here's where the party's at! Hi, Devan, how you doing, girl?" Matt walked up and gave me a big bear hug.

"Careful big fella. Those are my ribs rubbing together!" He put me down and tried to look apologetic. "I hope you're gentler with your boyfriends."

"I've tried working with him, trust me," Marti said, joining our circle, "but he's uncontrollable sometimes." They had a bond between them I envied…a loose, loving deeply trusting relationship you don't often see between a man and a woman. Because there was no sexual tension, Matt and Marti could enjoy their relationship together for what it was, a true friendship.

Matt asked, "Where's Corin?"

"She's over in the bushes looking for Emily."

"She's really freaked out about that asshole Joe. I never should have let her marry that guy." His demeanor darkened.

"I'm pretty sure you couldn't have stopped them, Matt, even if you'd been in town at the time," Marti said, something she'd probably told him more than once before. "Stop beating yourself up about it, there's nothing you could have done to prevent it. She was very much in love with Joe and he was very much in love with innocent, young Corin."

"Yeah well, it still pisses me off. And no one can tell me he loves her. He hit her so hard she was in the hospital for three days. That's not love in my book."

"No, in your book spanking and tying up are perfectly okay. Punching not okay. I've seen the pictures, thank you." Marti shook her head and turned her attention to me. "We just heard about Cleo and we tried calling Alex but the background noise in the hospital made it impossible to hear her. We heard her say 'Devan' several times and something about surgery? Broken bones? Skull fracture? Sounds horrible."

"Yes, it's pretty bad. The fire department had to cut her out of her car. I don't know how bad it is but it doesn't sound good to me."

"She's tough, just like Alex. It'll be okay. I'm sure of it," Matt said. Sometimes if you say things with enough conviction they come true.

"I hope so. I wanted to stay with Alex in the hospital but there were so many family members there I just didn't feel she needed me."

"You could have stayed. Alex would've liked that. She's very fond of you," Marti said.

"Oh, I didn't realize you knew Alex," I said.

"Yes, I've been going to her gym since she opened but I knew her before that."

"What do you mean she's very fond of me?" I wanted to know.

"From listening to her talk about you...that's the impression I get."

"Anyway, we might head on over to the hospital in a couple of days once Cleo's out of immediate danger, if you want to join us, Devan," Matt offered.

"Yeah, I would like that. Just give me a call when you're ready." Marti hadn't answered my question but I let it go.

Corin came back around and joined us. "I found her. She's just playing in her fort with a few dolls," Corin said. "I enjoy watching her play."

"I like how she plays with dolls and builds forts. You've done a great job with her Corin. She's a cute little girly tomboy," Marti commented.

"I don't know how much of that came from me but I'm grateful for her. She's my little angel," Corin said with love in her voice.

I added, "She's a doll."

"I think she got her imagination from her Uncle Mattie. He never built forts but he did build department stores in our mother's closet," Corin said.

Marti said with a laugh, "That sounds just like the Mattie we know and love."

"Wow, in the closet playing with women's clothes from an early age? Why am I not surprised?" Our little foursome stood around, gently teasing Matt until Corin took her leave. Matt and Marti, promising they'd call, went with Corin, leaving me alone in the backyard.

CHAPTER TWENTY-TWO

We were all ready for the drive over to the hospital a couple of days later. The three of us piled into Marti's car, a dark green, older Volvo station wagon. In the waiting room, I was surprised to see it was still wall-to-wall humans, we found Alex propped up in a chair fast asleep. I walked over to her and she stirred and opened her eyes.

"I turned around and you were gone," Alex said in the way of a hello.

"I felt you needed to be with family. How is Cleo?"

"She's much better. She's not as bad as we feared. She didn't fracture her skull after all, and there's very little internal bleeding. The doctors said she did great in surgery when they put her leg back together. I think Tony's in with her now. At least he was before I fell asleep."

"That's wonderful, Alex! I've been so worried about her."

"I'm sorry. I should have called you a couple days ago."

"Don't be silly."

"Thanks for coming out here. You didn't have to." She stood up and hugged me. The gratitude in her eyes pulled at my heart. "Oh, here comes Tony."

Tony came in to the waiting room and hugged Frank, his mom-in-law Pua, and said, "Cleo's been moved to a regular room!" A cheer went up in the small crowd, a tired but ecstatic cheer. Tony made his way over to us, grabbed Alex and smiled at me.

"Alex, Cleo is asking about you. She wants to see you again. She's worried about you." He held his hand out to me. "Hi, I'm Tony. You must be Devan." Formality taking over.

"Yes, hello, Tony. I hate that we're meeting under these circumstances, but it is nice to meet you."

"Why don't you go in with Alex? Cleo is looking so much better now and I'm sure she would love to meet you." He still had his arm around Alex's shoulders.

"I don't want to intrude. And I came with friends. I should get back with them." I looked around for Matt and Marti. Where did they go?

"M and M? They took Mom and Dad out for coffee. Seems like you have no choice but to hang with Alex, you poor kid." He laughed and sidestepped Alex's playful punch.

"Don't mind him," Alex said as Tony walked away. "He's the worst brother-in-law EVER!" She yelled so he could hear her. "Come on. Let's go see Cleo."

We wound down the corridor, toward Cleo's room and I felt overwhelmed. Hospitals gave me the jitters and I stayed close by Alex's side.

"How long have Cleo and Tony been married?"

"Let's see. Their oldest is six, so I'd have to say about eight years now. Why?"

"Just curious. You and Tony seem very close."

"Yeah, he's a great guy. I'm so glad Cleo married someone as easygoing as him. She dated a couple of losers briefly before she met Tony."

We entered the darkened room, listening for signs of life.

Cleo said from the dark, "There's my baby sister. Where have you been?"

"Cleo you are ninety-eight seconds older than me. I don't think that counts as being the big sister," Alex said. She walked over and turned on a small light in the corner, sat down next to the bed and gently took Cleo's hand. I stayed by the foot of the bed.

"Still, I was first. You know what that means."

"Mom saved the best for last?"

"You wish." Cleo turned her head and looked at me. "Oh, Alex. Tell me this is Devan."

"Yes. Hi, Cleo. How are you feeling?" I responded, surprised everyone seemed to know who I was.

"I feel pretty good," Cleo said dreamily.

"She's hopped up on the goofballs, this one," Alex whispered, pointing at Cleo and winking at me.

"You *are* beautiful, Devan."

"Well, thank you, Cleo. I was thinking the same thing about you."

"Yes, a much prettier, long-haired, voluptuous version of Alex."

"Don't forget older," Alex said.

"Oh, now I'm older huh?"

"That's enough out of you Cleo," Alex said, tucking in her blankets.

"Why don't you invite Devan to go with you to Maui like we talked about yesterday?" Alex froze in the act of shuffling sheets and I froze in the act of breathing. "With these broken ribs and all the hardware in my leg, I can't go anywhere but home. The way you go on and on about Devan—who else would you ask?"

"Oh, Cleo. I will give you anything to stop talking, please. I doubt Devan would want to go to Maui with me. We just met."

"Don't be silly. Wouldn't you love to go to Maui, Devan?"

"Yes I would love to go to Maui. But..." I was merely humoring Cleo, high as she was on painkillers.

"Done deal. You two go to Maui and have a great time," Cleo exclaimed, and promptly fell asleep.

"Wait…" Alex and I said at the same time.

"She floated away. She could be out for a while," Alex said. She looked across the bed at me. "Please don't listen to her. She's really high right now. I'm not sure what she's talking about."

"Sounds like you've been talking about me and not just with Cleo."

"I may have casually mentioned you to a few people."

"A few?"

"You're the new person in our little community. Excuse me for finding you interesting." I didn't know how to respond to that so I decided to let it go.

"Isn't that odd? Going to Maui together?"

"Well, the tickets are bought and paid for and we buy the cheapest tickets possible so I can't get a refund on them or change the date. Unfortunately, neither of us bought travel insurance. So it's use it or lose it."

"You can't be serious," I said.

"Well, it couldn't hurt to think about it."

"I'm sure you have a number of friends you would rather take with you."

"None I can think of at the moment," Alex replied after thinking about it for a second or two. "Just let me know if you don't want to go."

"I'll think about it."

"If it helps, the only thing you'll have to pay for is food. We'll be staying with my cousin, Kai, who's housesitting for a family living on the mainland during the fall. He sent me pictures of the house and it's amazing! It's such a big house you could have your own wing, if you wanted."

"I'll think about it. When exactly is it?" I said again.

"It's in a couple of months during Thanksgiving, so that wouldn't interfere with school or anything. Not that I've thought about it," she said laughing.

"I really don't think I should go, Alex. That's a little weird."

"Okay, just hold your answer until you thoroughly think about it. There's no rush. Can you stay with me now for a while or do you have to go?"

"I can stay with you."

We went back out to the waiting room and were quickly enveloped by Alex's family. I was introduced to grandma and grandpa, cousins, aunts and uncles, all on Frank's side. After a few minutes, Alex grabbed my hand and brought me over to her mother. Pua was tall and thin and looked just like her girls. She was wearing a flowered dress under a sweater and sandals and looked like she had just stepped off the beach to meet me. Pua ignored my handshake, pulling me into a loving hug I never wanted to leave.

"Devan, it's so nice to finally meet you." As she pulled away she held my face in her hands. "Alex has told me so much about you. You're a teacher at the middle school?" I couldn't really believe Alex had nothing better to talk about than me to her family and friends. What was going on here?

"Okay, Mom. Don't scare the poor lady."

"No, Alex, it's okay. I don't scare that easily. Yes, ma'am. I'm the new art teacher at Marbury."

"Please, call me Pua." She let go of my face and settled her hands with mine.

"Thank you, Pua, I will." We sat down on a couch and Alex wandered off to talk with her dad.

"Alex tells me you moved out here recently from Texas. But you're originally from Seattle, is that right?"

"Yes."

"Why didn't you move back to Seattle? Aren't your parents still there?"

"My parents live in Federal Way but my job is here."

"Your parents must have missed you, when you were so far away in Texas. I know I missed the girls when they went away to college. Florida! Can you imagine? That is *so* far away."

"My family isn't as close as your family. I think my parents were a little relieved when I moved away." I looked around the room surprised that everyone was still there.

"Oh, I don't believe that. No parent is relieved when their child moves away. Have you seen them since you've been back?"

"No, I haven't yet." I now felt like the worst child on the planet. How could I have not visited my family? "You must think I'm an awful person."

"No! My dear, Devan, I see nothing but goodness in you." She patted my hand and looked over at her husband. "Frank and I were drawn together because of our love of family. Everyone in this room welcomed me with open arms when Frank married me. They were loving and supportive of me during my time of transition when I moved here from the islands. They made my life so much easier."

"Mom! Hey! I think Dad wants to talk with you," Alex pleaded.

"Okay." She laughed and looked me in the eyes. "It was a pleasure meeting you Devan."

"Thank you, ma'am," I said before I realized. "I mean…Pua."

"Please come to the house and have dinner with me and Frank. You can bring Alex along if she's not too busy for her parents." She looked at Alex with so much love, I had to look away.

"Very funny, Mom." Alex helped her mother up and hugged her. "I love you, Mom. Now go."

"Okay, okay. Bye, Devan."

"Goodbye, Pua."

Alex sat down beside me and released a deep breath. "I'm sorry about that. My mom always says just a little too much. I hope she didn't make you uncomfortable."

"No. Not at all. Your family's so different from mine, but in a good way. My family was never demonstrative. We never hugged or said 'I love you.' It's a wonderful change to be around people who aren't afraid to show their love for each other. It's a little overwhelming, but nice."

"Well, if you think Dad's family is a little overwhelming, just wait until you meet Mom's family. In Hawaii."

"Oh really? I'm meeting both sides of your family already? I didn't realize we were dating." I was trying to be funny but it came out with a serious tone.

"What? No, no. I was just making conversation, that's all."

"Okay." I would take her word for it, although I was curious to know why everyone around Alex seemed to know me already.

"Yeah, they are *all* about being a family, everywhere I go when I'm in Maui. It's really great to be around them too." She rubbed her eyes and yawned, her lack of sleep these past couple of days catching up with her.

"Why don't you go home and sleep? You look like you could drop at any minute."

"I don't want to leave yet. I want to be here." She looked at me with her raccoon eyes and gave me a tired half smile.

"That's a good idea. I'll just leave you with your family." I looked around for my ride. Where were Matt and Marti?

"You can't leave."

"Why can't I leave, Alex?"

"Because I need a pillow." She turned and lay down, spread out on the couch with her head on my thigh.

"Oh…kay." Not knowing what to do with my hands, I rested one on the table next to me and the other on her hip. Her breathing deepened and she fell asleep. I sat that way for a couple of hours with Alex's family bringing me water and snacks and asking me about my life. Not in an intrusive way, more of an "I want to get to know you better" way. I could see what Pua was talking about with Frank's family. I felt like they cared about me, like they valued me as a person, like they were thrilled I had come into their lives. I didn't understand why, but could get used to it.

CHAPTER TWENTY-THREE

While sitting at my desk, waiting for class to begin on Monday, I thought about my future. There was a lot going on, almost too much. My encounter with Kelly had left me reeling emotionally. I wasn't sure how to handle my feelings for her. Alex was making it worse, with her invitation to Maui. To be fair, it was Cleo that asked, but Alex didn't laugh it off like I thought she would. She may think the better of it once the turmoil of the hospital settled down.

I took my lunch break with Linda, my favorite part of the day. I told her about dinner and the "encounter" with Kelly (my heat rising as we spoke, just thinking about it), Cleo's accident and, of course, the unlikely possibility of going to Maui with Alex. So much in so little time—life was funny like that. You could go weeks without anything really interesting happening and then, the next week, you didn't have time to sit and take a breather.

"I'm not going to say a word about you not being ready to get involved with anyone right now what with the pain of Steph leaving. I hope you realize how hard it is for me *not* to say anything."

"Yeah, thanks for not mentioning that. And I'm not 'in a relationship' with Kelly. We're just dating," I said.

"Okay. That's a little more than what I'd call dating but who am I?"

"Maybe, but I can handle it, okay?" I thought about it for a minute, faltering in my conviction. "Why? Do you think I'm going too far too fast?"

"It's none of my business so at any time you can tell me to stop and I will," Linda said.

"Well, when you put it like that, please stop."

"Just hear me out okay, Devan?" I got the feeling she wasn't going to stop, so I let her proceed. "Kelly is a known player."

Linda continued, "Kelly has been with a lot of women just for the sake of being with a lot of women. Do you know what I mean?"

"Do I want to?"

"From what you've told me about Steph, and you haven't told me much, but from what you've told me Kelly and Steph both seem to be saleswomen. Maybe closing the deal is what they're into."

"Kelly is nothing like Steph. She's helping me forget about Steph, especially after what happened after dinner."

"Is Kelly making you forget about Steph or just replacing her in your heart? Now, I'm not telling you how to live your life, but just think about that for a while," Linda said.

"I will, thanks. I think. Do you really think I would date someone like Steph so soon after Steph left me? Do you think I'm confusing the two of them?"

"That's all I'm going to say," she said, and then added, "sometimes the hardest things to see are things going on right in front of us...to us."

I would have to chew on Linda's advice for a while. "So what do you think about Maui?"

"I just think it's a little weird. How did it come about that Alex invited you to Maui with her? She always goes with Cleo."

"Cleo not only broke her leg, but broke three ribs as well. She can't travel and it was Cleo who suggested Alex and I go to Maui together. Alex thought it was weird too."

"Oh, well, that's a hard decision then. Maybe you should ask Ronnie's opinion. She thinks Alex is also a player, remember?"

"Right. I'll have to think about that one. Maui might not even happen. Alex will probably think of someone better to go with. Or she might not want to leave Cleo. I could just go without her, I guess. Ha! Wouldn't that be funny?"

"Oh, she'll go. Trust me," Linda said with a smile.

CHAPTER TWENTY-FOUR

I stopped by the gym after work to talk with Alex about Maui. No sense going on and on about something that might not even happen. Alex was deep in her sales pitch for the gym with a client. I went through to lift even though my new friend Pam was nowhere to be found. I warmed up a little, stretched a little and started my upper body workout with the bench press.

"You know, Devan, you're supposed to always have a spotter when doing movements like this right?" Alex had materialized out of thin air, sneaking up on me, hands on her hips, startling me.

"Yes, I know the rules. I couldn't find Pam and I feel weird asking someone I don't know to spot me. It always sounds like a horrible pickup line, 'Hey, baby come ova here and spot me a little!' Plus, I do things all the time I shouldn't be doing."

Alex walked around until she was hovering over me, near my head, ever the vigilant spotter, waiting for me to become trapped under the immense weight I was lifting. I was so glad I had put the ten pounders on the bar. They didn't look quite as wimpy as the five pounders. Alex asked, "What things?"

"How's your sister?" Not to change the subject or anything. I really wanted to know.

"She's doing remarkably well. I saw her this morning. She still looks beat up but she seems to be doing really well. It's going to take a while for her ribs to heal and even longer for her leg but she feels much better now. We both do. What things do you do that you shouldn't be doing?"

"I'd tell you but ladies don't speak of such things," I said.

"Oh my. Have you been naughty, Devan?"

"Are you still going to Maui?" As I brought the bar slowly down to my chest, Alex stood, legs apart, leaning over, hands hovering near the bar, ready to grab it when needed. She was concentrating on what she was doing, not answering right away. It caused me to hesitate, the bar suspended over my chest.

"Do you need me to grab the bar?" She had already tightened her grip on it.

"No," I said. "You don't have to grab anything."

"The trip isn't for a couple of months," she explained, letting go of the bar. "Cleo is looking so much better today and she's insisting that you and I go. I'm not as worried about her now. I've decided I'm definitely going."

"That's good to hear. I haven't decided yet. I just wanted to see if you were still going." I moved from the bench press to bicep curls. Alex moved behind me, touching my elbows, showing me how to lock my arms to maximize the workout on the desired muscle groups. She reached around with her left hand, placing it on my chest just below my neck. She placed her right hand on the small of my back and proceeded to explain the importance of good posture with all movements, her skin never breaking contact with mine, our eyes fixed on each other's. "Can you turn the fan on, Alex? I'm getting a little hot here." I could feel the heat rising to my face.

"Sure, yeah, let me get on that," Alex said. She pulled out the fan, which had been tucked away against the wall, aimed it toward me, turned it on and walked back over to the front desk. That's what I needed, a little cool air coming my way. Yes indeed.

Alex yelled from the counter, "Just let me know your final answer okay?"

"I'll do that," I said. Confusing times...I was intrigued by my feelings for Lori. And almost overwhelmed by Kelly and everything associated with her. But Alex—where did I begin? I knew, without hesitation, what both Lori and Kelly wanted from me. Maybe not specifics but I definitely knew the direction I was taking with those two. Alex though? I had no idea what she wanted from me. I looked up to see her smiling and waving at me. Was she being nice or was she toying with me? Did she want anything more than sex from me?

If I looked deep down, I thought Alex was playing with me because I was the newest person in town. I got the feeling she would tire of me quickly. I wasn't sure why I felt this way, but I did. I'd give Alex an answer in the next few days, so I could stop thinking about it, but was almost one hundred percent sure I wouldn't be going to Maui with her. I just didn't think it was a good idea. I couldn't see any good reason to go. I just wouldn't go.

CHAPTER TWENTY-FIVE

Matt was one of the most genuine people I had ever met. He would tell you exactly how he was feeling, holding nothing back, sometimes sharing a little too much information. One day he snuck into the teachers' lounge to have lunch with Linda and me. He brought pizza and soda, delighting us with stories of his prowls over the weekend. Vancouver seemed to be the smallest community in the States, and Matt and Linda jumped right in to the local gossip.

"Oh Matt, it's been too long! Ronnie and I *really* need to go out and have some fun. We've been way too serious together lately. Why don't you stop by the house later and we can make plans for a night out? You too, Devan, of course."

"Will do," Matt replied.

"Sounds like fun," I said.

"So Devan...how's Kelly? Is it getting serious?" Matt inquired.

"Yes, I think it is getting serious. I really like her."

"Oh, good. I hope it works out for you. Whoever you choose to be with."

"What does that mean?" I wondered out loud.

"He means Kelly or Lori. Right, Matt?"

"Yes! Lori or Kelly or whoever, doesn't matter." Matt switched his focus from me to Linda. "Do you think you could get a sitter for Friday night, Linda?"

"Sure, both our immediate families live here and Grammas just love to watch them."

"Well, I've got to run, ladies," Matt said, kissing us each on the cheek, "I've got work to do."

"He's a lot of fun," I said after Matt was out of hearing range.

"Yeah, he's a great person to hang around with. He seems to be just thrilled to be alive. I wish he could share some of his happy genes with his sister. Corin and I know each other but not well. I feel bad for her. She's always stressed out and unhappy." Linda leaned forward on the table. "Maybe you should talk with her, Dr. Scott. Maybe she'll open up to you."

"I'm not in that business anymore, Linda. I don't want the relationship Corin and I have to be one of therapist and patient. I like things just the way they are. And I don't think Corin necessarily needs therapy. She needs to get her ex-husband out of her life. Once that happens she'll probably feel a lot better about things."

"True. I just wish there was something we could do for her."

"Me too."

"Hey, why don't you bring her and Emily over to our house one day? Cameron would love to have a girl to hang out with. How old is she again?"

"She's eleven, so not much older than Cameron."

"Yeah, bring them over," Linda said.

"Why don't *you* just call her up and ask?"

"That feels weird. I think it would be more comfortable for everyone if it was from you. Kind of a casual 'hey, I'm going over to Ronnie and Linda's. You two want to come along?'"

"Okay, that's a good idea."

"See? That's why you keep me around. I'm full of good ideas."

"Full of something," I said quietly. If I had said something like that around my brother he would have given me nothing but grief.

"What was that?"

"Nothing my friend. Nothing at all." Our bell sounded, shattering our thoughts, forcing us out into the hallway to make our way to our respective classrooms.

As a parting question, Linda asked, "So, *are* you seeing Kelly again?"

"Yes, we're going to the new Vietnamese restaurant. You're not going to tell me not to are you?"

"No! I said my piece and now I'm leaving it up to you."

I responded, "Good. Thank you."

CHAPTER TWENTY-SIX

Later that day I stopped by the store on the way home, before going over to Linda's, and ran into Ronnie in the parking lot.

"Hi, Devan! How are you? Linda said you and Matt were coming over for dinner and I need a few things."

"You really don't have to do too much for me so if you want me to grab a rotisserie chicken or two that would be just fine."

Ronnie replied, "Don't be silly, I'd love to make dinner for you. Really, what's two more people added to our brood of five? Don't worry about it."

"Okay, I just don't want you to feel like you have to."

"Not a problem. How's Alex?"

I said, "She's doing much better now that Cleo is in a regular room. Have you been to see her?"

"No, I didn't want to intrude. I went to see Alex at the gym this morning. She seemed fine, but you know how she is...keeps everything bottled up inside." She smiled at me like I should know this fact. Ronnie had, after all, been in a relationship with her, but she was just a friend to me. It's not like Alex and I spent a lot of time together.

"Yes, I think she's doing better."

"Linda tells me you're dating Kelly, is that right?"

"Yes, we've been on a couple of dates, nothing too serious."

"Well, good luck with that," Ronnie responded.

"Good luck?"

"Yeah, she's a lot like Alex. Not one for commitments."

"Oh, that's okay. I'm not one for commitments at the moment either. I'll be just fine."

"I've got to run, Devan. I'll see you in a little while. Say hi to Alex for me."

"I will if I see her. Nice to see you too, Ronnie," I said.

Driving home, I thought about what Ronnie had said. She seemed a little too focused on Alex but maybe I was just reading too much into her choice of words. Was she still hung up on Alex? Or was she just a concerned friend reaching out? I knew I really shouldn't dwell on those things but I couldn't help it. I decided to just ask Alex outright what she thought about it the next time I saw her.

* * *

"Why did you and Ronnie break up?" I asked with no warning and no hello. Okay, so I'd decided to drive right over to the gym and ask her.

"Oh, okay that makes sense. Ronnie huh?" She shook her head and smiled. "Ronnie expressed her desire for marriage and kids after we'd been together not even a month. I thought that was a bit soon. I liked her but her intensity was too much for me."

"She is a little intense but to hear her say it you were afraid of commitment."

"Well, after only a month, I wasn't ready to commit. Not even a little, and I really don't think I want kids *at all*. I don't think I'm mature enough for kids...or I don't want to be at any rate."

"I know how you feel."

"And why are you so interested?"

"I can't help it. The psychologist in me is dying to know. Ronnie tells me one thing and I see another. I can't help but be intrigued."

"Ronnie imagines things. I didn't even realize we were dating until we were a couple of weeks into it. I know I shouldn't have slept with her but I couldn't help myself. I was really young and sex was a new thing for me, something to play with and explore. I hurt her because I didn't realize how she felt. *I* thought we were having a good time. *She* was planning our wedding. Seriously, I had no idea what was going on in her head."

"It seems to be working for her and Linda, I guess."

"Yeah, most of the time they seem very happy together. I wish them the best of luck," Alex said. "Are you going to work out now? Do you need a spotter? I'm available at the moment."

"No, I've got other plans but thanks for the info," I said making my way to the door.

"Oh, I see how you are. You pump me for information then discard me like yesterday's guacamole."

"Yep. That's me. It's what I do," I said with a smile, stopping at the door. "I'll see you later, Alex."

"I'll be right here waiting for you, Devan." What a goofball. Waiting for me. I wish someone *would* wait for me. Oh well, just one more thing to add to my Wishful Thinking list.

CHAPTER TWENTY-SEVEN

I pulled up to Linda and Ronnie's house, behind what I assumed was Matt's car...a shiny, dark red Jeep Wrangler. I could picture Matt in the Jeep, with the top off, wind whipping his short hair, grinning like a little devil, men falling all over themselves trying to ride shotgun. I pulled the two bottles of wine from the trunk (you never know when red or white is appropriate) and made my way to the front porch. I could hear the laughter inside, mostly Matt's.

Ronnie answered the door with a glow on her cheeks and a smile. "Devan! Long time no see. Come on in. Linda and Matt are in the kitchen. Oh, more wine. My two favorites: white and red."

"Thanks." It was quiet on the way back to the kitchen. "What, no kids tonight?"

"They'll be here in a little bit. They're with friends at the community center," Ronnie said.

"Since neither of us are swimmers and the kids love to swim, our next-door neighbors take them whenever they can," Linda said as she pulled out a chair for me. I smiled at Matt and poured myself a glass of wine. It felt comfortable here in the kitchen waiting for dinner and I had that sense again, the one that tugs at my heart, asking the questions I couldn't answer, evoking thoughts I didn't want to deal with. I decided the best way to deal with my feelings was to drown them in wine. Problem solved.

"I hope everyone will stay for dinner. We're having taco salads," Ronnie said, her back to us as she worked at the stove. "This is the best way to get vegetables into the kids. Nothing says yummy to them like ground beef, cheese and ranch dressing. So I won't win Mother of the Year. I still hold out hope for next year!"

"I can't stay long, girls, I have plans in a bit with a new friend, Jose," Matt said with a wistful look on his face. "What shall we do about Friday? You want to hit the clubs with me?"

"I do! I do!" said Ronnie, looking very excited about the prospect.

"Me too!" I chimed in.

"That sounds like a blast. Count me in," Linda said.

"Great. I'll see you girls at nine, at The Tav, okay?"

I asked, "At nine really?"

"I know, it's a little early but I figure it'll be quieter early in the evening so we can talk and mingle with everyone." Yeah, that's what I meant. *Way* too early for me. "We'll start there and move our way around the area. I'm gonna go and shower before my date." Matt rose to leave when Ronnie cut him off.

"Sit down, Matt, and let me feed you before you go. You need some protein for your shenanigans. Sit down."

"Okay, Mom, I'll eat. Just don't spank me!" He was still laughing when Ronnie placed his dinner in front of him.

"If I didn't think you'd enjoy it so much, I *would* spank you," Ronnie said with a glint in her eye. "Everyone else, help yourselves." Linda and I jumped up and did just that. I savored every bite. Ronnie had a way of making everything taste better than it should. She cut all the veggies up and piled them into separate bowls, years of kids ingrained into her routine, making it easy to customize one's salad.

When the kids returned, Matt jumped up and relinquished his seat, making a run for the door. The kids were wound up from swimming, burning calories at an alarming rate, hungry beyond words. They devoured their salads. After eating, the kids cleared off their dishes and, with homemade cookies in hand, rumbled down the stairs to play. I had to laugh. They seemed to have only one speed. I promised myself to sneak in one night to see them sleeping, just to make sure they actually did have an off switch.

* * *

I really wanted to make an impression on Kelly. I wanted her to look at me like no one else did, with a longing she couldn't hide. I wore a short skirt, a tight-fitting blouse and brand-new two-inch heels. It was raining so my sexy outfit was hidden beneath a raincoat. I would have to wait until we were inside the restaurant to see the look on Kelly's face. I arrived there, early as usual, and sat down at the bar waiting for her. I looked around and was surprised to see Alex. She was *everywhere* in town.

Alex was with Cathy, a friend of Matt's I'd met at Ladies' Night Out. I was deciding whether to say hello or not when Alex looked up, caught my eye and waved at me. I waved back and smiled, a little unnerved.

The hostess let me know my table was ready and told me that when my friend arrived we would be seated immediately. I ordered a drink and waited. I didn't start worrying until my third drink. I tried calling Kelly and her phone went immediately to voice mail. Crap. It appeared I'd been stood up.

Alex and Cathy got up from their table and waved a goodbye. I mustered up a smile, which died on my face when Alex turned to go and put her hand on the lower part of Cathy's back, the very low part of Cathy's back, the warm, comfortable spot where Alex could guide her out the door. What was *that* about? Much too friendly for a casual dinner.

The hostess came by and asked how I was doing. I told her my friend had called and she had to cancel. Another little white lie I could live with. Could she just seat me? I ate dinner alone, savoring the food, trying to forget how angry I felt. How could she want me so badly one minute and then the next not even bother to call. Maybe Linda was right. Maybe Kelly was a souped up version of Steph. Maybe she had gotten what she wanted and had moved on. I couldn't believe someone could be that shallow. Maybe *Kelly* had been in a car accident. Maybe I was sitting here pissed for no reason, Kelly being injured or hurt in some way.

After dinner the thought of going home and sitting around angry didn't appeal. Needing a friend I called Lori, and was thrilled when she said she was at a stopping point in her work. Since we'd both eaten already we decided on going to see *Bridesmaids*, which seemed a fitting balm to my bruised ego.

The movie was hilarious, funny in a very crass way, touching in a laughable way. Lori and I really connected during the movie—laughter has a way of doing that—and we walked out talking excitedly. "We'll have to rent it when it comes out on DVD and watch it again. I think I laughed through half of the dialogue." We walked back to Lori's duplex and sat on the stairs of her little stoop. She looked at me with amusement.

"What?"

"You have a great laugh, almost like a little kid's. Do you know what I mean?"

"No. Sounds like you're saying I'm immature," I said with a laugh.

"No, silly. When you let go and really laugh, you light up a room with your happiness."

"Oh," was all I could think to say. "Thanks. And thanks for coming out with me."

"You're welcome," Lori replied. "Thanks for pulling me away from my work. I needed to clear my head a little."

We sat on the stoop for a while talking, laughing, giving and getting. We talked until I realized we had leaned into each other and were touching shoulders and holding hands. Lori invited me in for a drink but I declined. I didn't feel exclusive with Kelly but I wasn't sure sleeping with two women at the same time was really who I wanted to be. I was very tempted, though. I said goodnight and left.

Moving to Vancouver was the best thing I could have done. Not only did I find a job but I found my life again. Where had it been all these years?

CHAPTER TWENTY-EIGHT

Was it just me, or was the world becoming an exclusive community of ironic hipsters I couldn't quite follow? Much of the time, I had no idea what the kids at school meant but they made me smile. I felt the need to hit the gym after the last bell, needed to sweat out my elderly vibes and replace them with hip ones. I kept checking my phone, hoping to see a missed call from Kelly. I finally called and left her an amusing message to which I got no reply. I guess I was the only one who realized how funny I was.

Alex was alone at the front counter. She seemed very happy, glowing really.

"Hey Devan! What are you up to this fine day?"

"No good. How was dinner last night?"

"We had a great meal. I like that place."

"I didn't know you and Cathy were friends."

"Cathy and I go way back, hooking up every now and then for something different. Cathy, she's a wild one," Alex said her eyes glazing over.

I asked, "What happened to 'I determined I needed to spend some time alone'?"

"Is that what I said?"

"Yes, verbatim," I replied.

"Verbatim huh? Well, I get tired of being alone every night. Stacy and I broke up months ago so I'm not cheating on anyone. And it's not like we got married. We just had sex. Wild, uninhibited, up-all-night sex," Alex said with a smile.

"Oh, no details please. I'm thrilled to see you letting it all hang loose, with not a care in the world, fulfilling every carnal desire." I wasn't sure what the hell I was talking about.

"It sure was thrilling last night. And what are you so upset about? Why do you care what I do? Didn't you have fun with... whatshername?"

"Kelly," I replied.

"Yes, your new friend Kelly. You two have been having a lot of fun recently, haven't you?"

"That's none of your business," I said. I could feel the heat rising up from my chest, washing over my face, lighting me up like a Christmas tree. I had to lean over slightly, with my hip on the counter, to keep from swaying. I didn't feel the need to tell Alex that Kelly had stood me up. I didn't want to hear and see any sympathy from someone who'd been up all night having sex.

"That means yes," Alex informed me.

"Why does it have to mean anything?" Not that *I* could talk. I attach meaning to every little thing. Hypocrisy: just one more weapon in my arsenal.

"Everything means something," Alex replied.

"Were you put on this Earth to annoy me?" I was more than a little irritated, especially since Alex appeared to find this whole conversation hilarious.

"Seems that way." She laughed, leaning on the counter from the exertion.

Well, that was enough of a warm-up for me so I got right down to lifting weights. I must say, that was the best workout I had ever had. I ended up shaky, having sweated through my clothes, collapsing in a pile in a corner. I would have stayed there for a while had I not remembered I was annoyed with Alex and wanted to leave. She gave me a big smile as I was leaving and I tried to return the sentiment, but it must have come out as a grimace because she laughed on my way out the door. Laugh it up, darling.

CHAPTER TWENTY-NINE

Friday night couldn't have come any faster. I just wanted to cut loose and enjoy myself, tired of my wobbly emotional life. I dolled up, hit the Prius and made my way to The Rainbow Tavern. I didn't know what to expect having never been out with the boys on a Friday night. I certainly wasn't expecting Alex to be there. She was just outside the entrance, leaning back against the wall, cowboyed up, looking for a good time.

"Hey, Devan. Nice to see you again." She was still wearing the laughter from the other day.

"Hi, Alex. What are you doing here? Come to find a few boys to play with? Give them some tips on how to score?" Settle down, Devan. No need to get catty.

"No. Matt asked me to come along. He thought I might enjoy a night out. Didn't he mention that to you? He said you'd be here."

"No. I don't recall being told anything. We really should stop meeting like this...seriously, how small is this town?"

"It's pretty small. So small this is the only gay bar in town. We'll have to go down to Portland to get a little variety. Are you up for staying out past your bedtime?" I would be more annoyed, had Alex's smile not been so genuine and infectious. Her barbs had a gentleness to them, almost like being hit with a feather. Instead of pushing me away tonight, her gentle ribbing brought me closer to her. "Does Austin have a big gay population?"

"It's pretty big, for Texas, I guess. Steph and I didn't go out at all though so I have no idea really. Austin is a university town so there's a lot more going on there than in other parts of Texas."

"I've heard the U of T is pretty big but, come on...the Longhorns as a mascot? The Oregon State Beavers are a much better mascot, in my opinion," Alex said.

"Ha ha. Aren't you funny?"

"I'm trying to be."

"Yes, Alex, you *are* trying."

Unbeknown to us, Matt had just arrived. "Well, aren't you the cutest couple?" Alex and I had moved close together, our heads leaning in to each other. I took a step back and smiled at our guide for the evening. "Look what I found in the parking lot...a couple of lesbians calling themselves Linda and Ronnie. They were just milling about and I thought they had the look of people desperately needing a drink. Let's go, ladies!"

"I know *I* could use a drink," Linda responded.

Ronnie retorted, "Why don't you have a couple?" Linda and Ronnie kept a distance between them which looked both literal and figurative. Their body language was full of tension.

We walked into The Rainbow Tavern and I immediately noticed a different vibe than I had felt on girls' night. The music was different: deeper, stronger, more passion. The throbbing bass pulsated through everything but especially through the floor making it hard to walk in my heels. Without thinking, I slipped my hand around Alex's bicep. Her rock-hard bicep. She moved her hand up to her stomach flexing her arm for my benefit and amazement. It wasn't long before Matt found a group of his welcoming friends. There wasn't enough room for all of us to sit, leaving Alex, Matt and Linda standing. I believed this was Matt's preferred position, since it allowed him to show off his wares.

"I have an itch and I need some scratchin'!" Matt declared, walking off into the crowded dance floor which parted for him and closed up behind him in an intimate embrace.

"That's the great thing about gay men: without women to hold them back there's no reason not to have lots of sex," Alex said. "Now we women, we always supply reasons not to have sex. We could learn a thing or two from the guys. There's nothing wrong with pure lust."

"I agree with that," Ronnie said.

"We have three kids, you know! I get tired," Linda said. The tension I felt between them was now boiling over, the lid flung off into the crowd, nothing to stop the anger now.

"Um," I said, thinking it was a good idea to get out of their general vicinity, "Alex would you like to dance?"

"Love to." She grabbed my hand, pulling me into the mass of men. We moved with the song, shaking off the discomfort created by Ronnie and Linda's exchange. Alex leaned her head close to mine, our bodies almost touching, her breath on my neck, causing my heat to rise. "Yikes! That was uncomfortable."

"You could say that. I probably shouldn't even ask but do you know what's going on between them?" The tempo of the music changed, slowed down a bit, allowing me to put my hands on Alex's broad shoulders, allowing Alex to put her hands on my hips. I leaned my head down onto my hand as Alex brought her hands around to the small of my back. We fit perfectly.

"They don't seem as happy as they used to be. They haven't been socializing as much as they used to and they rarely come to the gym anymore. I don't see them as much but when I do they don't seem happy around each other."

"Oh, Alex. I hate that. I hope they can work it out."

"Me too."

We moved together, forgetting about the crowd, forgetting about others' problems. The feelings Alex invoked in me were confusing: she annoyed me most of the time, but every once in a while, like that moment, I had strong feelings for her, perhaps desire. I felt I could have stayed there forever, had Ronnie not found us.

"Linda and I are leaving. Apparently we have some issues we need to work on. You two have fun and don't pay any attention to us," Ronnie said.

"You know, couple's therapy works wonders for some," I said. I had to lean around Alex, to talk with Ronnie, unable to let go.

Ronnie asked, "Could you tell that to Linda?"

"Do I have to?"

"No. She probably won't listen to you either. She refuses to acknowledge our problems, insisting everything is perfectly fine," Ronnie said with sadness in her eyes.

"Hang in there, kid," Alex said. "It'll all work out."

"Thanks, Alex. See you two later." Ronnie left us alone and we went back to each other.

"Hang in there, kid?" I looked at Alex amused by her choice of words. "What about: 'It's always darkest just before the dawn'?"

"Don't laugh! I didn't know what to say! I was afraid she would start talking about their sex life. I don't want to hear about that, especially if it's bad," she said with a little shake of her head. "You used to be a therapist, why don't you help them?"

"I can't do that. First, I'm a teacher now not a therapist. Second, they're friends and so can't be clients. Third, I don't want to hear about their sex life any more than you do."

"I guess I can understand that."

"Well, I'm so happy you can guess," I said.

"And I'm happy you can count to three," she replied. Touché, damn her. The music picked up speed and we eased away until we were no longer touching. I'm not sure why I was so sensitive and immature around her. No one else made me lose my cool like Alex could.

Alex searched for Matt in the crowd. "Looks like it's just you and me Devan. Is that okay with you?"

"Yes. You aren't nearly as annoying as you normally are," I replied, wondering why I was being so childish with her. "Matt's standing over by the stage, working his magic, talking with another side of beefcake. I can spot that pink shirt of his from a mile away."

"Yeah, he's not having any problems tonight. I'm telling you, Devan, men have it easy. It's just sex to them. They have as much fun as they can and, when they get a little older, most settle down. But I bet they still have a lot of sex, more than us women do."

"You're all about the sex aren't you?" I asked. Alex slowed down a little, to ponder my question.

"Is it wrong I enjoy sex, so much?" She looked deep into my eyes making my heart flutter a little. It was getting *really* hot in there. Odd, as I wasn't even sure that I *liked* this woman. We had moved to the edge of the crowd, close to our table, close to breaking our bond.

"No, not at all," was the only answer I could think of at the moment. I really needed to sit down and catch my breath. When I turned to go, Alex grabbed my hand, insisting I keep dancing. "Alex, I can't. I have to climb down from these shoes, little miss 'I'm fine, I wore men's shoes to this party.'"

"That sounds like a personal problem."

"Very personal for my feet," I said, and walked over to the table. I *did* wish I had brought an extra pair of shoes for dancing but I'd survive. I swear I'm tough.

"You didn't have to get all dressed up just for tonight. Who did you think you would run into? Were you hoping someone special would show up?"

"No. I'm an adult. I like to get dressed up for going out, no matter what the event. If it's important enough for me to go, I like to dress like it's important. I don't want to look like I parked my skateboard out front and decided to go to the book reading or whatever it may be."

"Even though technically we live in Vancouver, Devan, this is the Portland area...we generally don't do things just for looks. If I pay the admission price for something that alone should be enough to show I care about the event. It shouldn't matter what I wear. I'm there aren't I?"

"I can't change how I feel just because it would make you more comfortable, Alex. This is who I am and how I was raised. Seattle can't be *that* much different. Can it?"

"Oh, yes it is. Portland and Seattle are two entirely different cities. I've always thought of Seattle as the stuffy, older conservative sibling while Portland is the cooler, slightly unruly, much younger child."

"Well, then don't be surprised when I show up in torn jeans and a tank top to go to the theater with you."

"Are you asking me out?" Her eyes got wide, her hands moved up to cup her face. "Because it kinda sounds like you're asking me out!"

"No! I wasn't asking you out."

"That's what it sounded like to me."

"Can we just dance some more please?"

"Okay. Dance now, date later," she said, very pleased with her witty self, her smugness not ruining her good looks, her beautiful smile. I decided to concentrate on my annoyance with Alex and not on my sore feet. We saw Matt occasionally, usually with a very attractive young man close by, a look of satisfaction on Matt's glowing face. He was entirely in his element. I grew tired of dancing and trading jibes with Alex and looked for a reason to go home.

"I need to go, Alex. You're right. It's way past my bedtime."

"Can I give you a lift?"

"No, I drove. Thanks for keeping me upright all night."

"You're welcome. It was my pleasure. Not long until Maui! I can't wait. Did you make a decision about going?"

I hadn't really thought about it but, looking up into Alex's eyes, I made a fast decision. "I would kick myself for years if I didn't jump on this opportunity, Alex. And it would kill me to have to listen to your stories about it for the next few months. Yes. I'd love to go."

"We'll have a great time, Devan. You won't be disappointed. I promise," Alex said.

"That reminds me—how is Cleo doing?"

"She's doing much better. Her ribs are healing as expected. But she'll be in the hospital another week or so because they're worried she'll injure her leg if they let her go home. It was a *really* nasty fracture, and they often don't heal well. She had a pin driven into her fibula and multiple pins and screws implanted into her tibia. I'm not sure when those will come out, if ever." As we talked Alex moved closer to me and we started slowly dancing again.

"You could go see her. If she didn't have such a bad leg I'm sure she'd have climbed the walls by now."

"Okay, I'll try and make it out there. I really have to go home now, though."

"Stay with me please."

"I can't. I have to go." I pulled away from her and smiled. "Thanks for the dance."

"My pleasure."

She walked me to my car and watched me leave, waving in my rearview mirror until I couldn't see her anymore.

CHAPTER THIRTY

I awakened not knowing what woke me, just knowing it was *not* good. I tried to gauge what time it was since looking over at my clock would have required turning over. From the lack of sunlight I decided it was too early to get up. I closed my eyes, drifting off to sleep, when I heard it again. Was that a scream?

I threw on some clothes, then threw on some more, boots and a jacket, and hurried down the steps. I hesitated at the bottom of the stairs not knowing where to turn when the scream came again. It sounded like a young girl. I ran to Corin's house. Please let Emily be okay.

Corin's bedroom window was open. Emily stood at the foot of the bed. She screamed again, causing me to scream as well. Joe Steiner, Corin's ex, was on his knees on the bed, on top of Corin, hitting her with his closed fists. He saw me at the window. I froze at the look on his face. He was going to kill them. My adrenaline, already in gear, jumped into overdrive. He leapt off the bed and ran toward me. My brain wouldn't release my body from where I was standing. Seemingly effortlessly, Steiner grabbed me and pulled me in through the window. He flung me on the bed and I landed with my head on Corin's knees.

"Corin!" She didn't move. I focused on protecting Emily. "Emily. Run!"

Steiner lunged at me, grabbed me by the hair and pulled me up. I saw the rage in his eyes. He pulled his arm back to hit me and I quickly jabbed him in the eye with my thumb. He yelled out and loosened his grip on my hair. When he brought his hand up to his face, I brought my knee up into his groin. I mostly hit thigh but I got him enough to cause him to gasp, let go and fall to the floor.

I turned to Emily who was rooted to her one spot. "Call nine-one-one. Now!" I pushed her out to the hall. She was in shock and moving on wooden legs. "Emily—now!" I wheeled around to help Corin, and Steiner lashed out at me with a six-inch hunting knife, aiming for my belly. I tried to twist sideways out of his way, but the knife skimmed the skin on my left side. I grabbed his hand and tried to pull the knife away from him. I kept twisting and fell to the floor, pulling him with me. He bounced off the bureau and let go of the knife. He fell on top of me and rolled off near the window. I grabbed the knife and jumped up. Steiner stood up, saw I had the knife and smiled. His right eye was blinking involuntarily, watery and red, the only thing moving on his body.

We stood like that, in a standoff, for a couple of seconds before Emily ran into the room. She stopped by her father and started yelling at him at the top of her lungs. "Stop hurting people!" Steiner looked confused when Emily started hitting him with her little fists. It was this distraction that saved my life.

Steiner's head whipped up when he heard the first siren. He placed his hand on Emily's head and pushed her out of the room. He looked at me with flaming eyes and swore at me. "You bitch! I'll see you later." He dove out the window and was gone. I ran behind him and closed and locked the window. Emily staggered back in and flung herself at me, crying and yelling.

"Emily. It's over. Come on." I held her and dragged her over to Corin.

"Mommy!" Emily yelled and untangled herself from me. She stumbled toward her mom and climbed up next to her. "Mommy?" Emily asked quietly this time.

Corin was still. Her face was bloody and bruised. She was still tangled in the sheets, only her head and arms visible. Her arms were already showing signs of heavy bruising. I couldn't wake her but she was breathing. The sirens were getting louder and more insistent.

"Stay with your mom, Emily. I'm going to look out front for the police." I had become too hot with my layers of clothing and pulled my coat off flinging it under the window.

The phone was lying in the hallway still connected to the dispatcher. I picked up the phone and said, "Hello?"

"What's going on, ma'am?" The dispatcher sounded professional.

"We need an ambulance."

"One's on the way. It should be there within a couple of minutes. Is the threat over?"

"Yes, he's left. I think it's over. We need an ambulance for Corin," I said as I made my way carefully over to the window afraid Steiner would jump out from the shadows and attack me.

"Are you sure he's gone?"

"I'm pretty sure. I saw him jump out the window." I reached the front window and looked out onto the street. No ambulance or police yet.

"Are you in the house?"

"Yes. Steiner left and the three of us are locked in the house." I reached up and touched the wound in my side, realizing I was bleeding. That was going to sting a little later.

"Stay where you are. The ambulance should be there in a moment."

"I can hear them. Can you tell the police that Steiner is gone? I don't want Emily terrified anymore."

"Yes, ma'am. I've told them the three of you are alone."

"Thank you."

"Stay on the line, please."

"Okay," I said, and promptly hung up. I flung the phone on the couch and went to make sure Emily was okay. She had curled up beside Corin, her little arm across Corin's chest and she was whispering, "It's okay, Mommy. He won't hurt you anymore. It's okay."

"Emily honey. The police are coming and it might get loud in here. When the emergency medical technicians get here you might have to move, okay?" I didn't know how to explain it but she was nodding her head, the haze in her eyes slowly dissipating.

"Why did Daddy do this? What did Mommy do?"

"Your mom didn't do anything and I don't know why your dad did this. I really don't know, Em."

"I don't understand." She was trying to wrap her eleven-year-old mind around the concept of brutality and failing.

"Neither do I. Stay with your mom." I ran back to the window in time to see Sam screech to a halt at the curb, jump out of her cruiser and run toward the door. I opened the door and stepped back for her to enter.

"In the bedroom Sam. He's gone now. Emily's with her mom."

"What happened, Devan?" she yelled as she went past me into the house. Steiner was the only thing I said. The look on her face was one of high alert mixed with grief. She searched the house and ran into the bedroom, cursing under her breath the whole time. "Emily, are you okay?" I heard her say as I walked out into the night, intent on pointing out the house to the EMTs. They pulled out their gear and ran toward the house.

"Ma'am. Sit on the stairs, please, so we can take a look at you," the kind-looking young man said as he set his bag down next to me. I followed his eyes to my side. Blood had soaked my clothing down my left side all the way to my knee. He quickly checked my pulse.

"No. I'm fine. It's not as bad as it looks. It's really just a scratch. I always bleed an excessive amount. I'm not sure why. There's a woman inside who is seriously injured. You can look at me later." Steiner's knife had hit me in the side but mostly got tangled up in all the clothing I was wearing. Thank heavens for layers.

"Okay, but don't go anywhere." He ran inside with his partner. I waited out front, sitting on the stairs, arms around my knees, waiting for the waves of shaking to cease. I had to move when the EMTs brought Corin out on a gurney. I stood on trembling legs, Sam there to catch me so I wouldn't fall. I leaned against her, cradled against her side. Emily had come out with them and she now hugged me from the front.

"I'm so glad you're here, Sam."

"I was going to get a bite to eat when I heard the address over the dispatch. I've called in that I'm here, but Burkov should be here any second." With that, Burkov screeched to a halt at the curb. They talked for a moment and he went inside. "I'm going to the hospital to make sure she's okay," Sam said. She loosened her grip on me and looked deep into my eyes. "Are you okay?"

"I will be." I looked down at Emily. "Yes. I'm fine. Go."

"I'll be back when she's settled in." And she was gone.

The EMTs had called for another ambulance to take care of me. I refused to get into it against the advice of the tech. I wouldn't leave Emily. I was bandaged up with a stern warning from the EMTs to go to the hospital as soon as I could to have my wound checked. I promised I would and Emily and I went into the house to sit. I answered questions from Burkov and the newly arrived detectives until Sam came back.

"How is Corin?" I asked, holding Emily against my good side.

"She's as good as can be expected, at the moment," Sam replied, sitting next to Emily on the couch. "I can't find Matt. Corin wanted Emily to stay with Matt but she knew he went out tonight."

"We went out dancing and drinking."

"Well damn. He could be *anywhere* then," Sam said.

"Yeah. He was just getting started when I left, right before midnight. What time is it now?"

"It's three."

"You haven't found Joe yet, have you?" I said, trying to be quiet with Emily still attached to me.

"No. He just went from a trespassing misdemeanor from the other night to a felony assault, though. We've put out a bulletin for him."

There were police everywhere. Vancouver was a quiet town unaccustomed to this kind of violence. It seemed like every cop in town was now parked out front of Corin's house. All the neighbors were out on their porches, wondering what was going on. Officers walked around asking if anyone saw or heard anything. Besides Sam, the four police I could remember were officers Adams and Burkov and detectives Rodriguez and Carter.

"Maybe you should call Linda. We were talking the other day, at the gym, about how fond she was of you. Stay with them for a while," Sam said, when it looked like things were wrapping up. "I can stay with Emily until we find Matt."

"Is there any way she can stay with me?" I looked down at the top of Emily's head.

"Let me call the hospital and see if one of the nurses can ask Corin. I'll be right back."

I called Linda and she was already up. Some people actually do wake up voluntarily before five a.m.

"Hi, Devan. Man, you sure are up early."

"I need your help."

"What can I do?" That's when I lost it. I got up from the couch, not wanting to upset Emily any more. I cried and in between sobs tried to explain what happened, but all I could manage was the general idea that I needed to stay with her and Ronnie for a few hours until I could talk with Matt or Corin. She agreed and told me I could stay as long as I needed to, why don't I bring some of my things over? She also said she'd put on another pot of coffee for me. Apparently, I sounded like someone who needed some coffee.

Officer Adams, in a small-town coincidence Sam's older brother, was kind enough to walk me to my apartment so I could pick up some things. There was no way I was staying at my place with that maniac on the loose. Until Steiner was caught, I was not going *near* Corin's house.

My cell phone rang. My jangled nerves responded with a start but when I checked the number I was relieved to see it was Matt.

"Hi, Matt." I tried to be calm but I started weeping again.

"Devan. What's going on? Sam left a message on my cell and said something about Corin being attacked, going to the hospital? Is Emily with you? What the hell happened?"

"Corin's alive, Matt. She's in the hospital. Emily is with Sam at the house. You need to come and be with Emily. Do you want me to take her to Ronnie and Linda's with me or should we meet you here?"

"Jesus Christ! Steiner is a steaming pile of shit. Did they catch him?"

"No. He ran before the police arrived. They're looking for him."

"Shit! I'll see you at Linda's."

Thanks to Sam, Emily and I made it to Linda's house, and only then I realized I should have changed my clothes. Linda nearly fainted when she saw the blood. Ronnie merely swore under her breath, sent Linda to get us some coffee and helped me take off a couple of layers. Emily wouldn't leave my side so I made her lie down on the couch, just for a minute, I told her and after she relaxed and we stopped talking about her mom, she was fast asleep.

Sam took me to the hospital to get a few stitches. I told her it was really just a scratch, and that I just bleed a lot. I was taken in immediately. It helps to bring a big, angry cop with you. My wound was superficial and the doctor inspected, cleaned and stitched within thirty minutes. I sat rigidly in the car on the ride back wishing I could relax just a little and doze. I was exhausted but still too amped to give into it.

When Sam dropped me off at Linda and Ronnie's house, Matt was there looking gray and harried, not unlike someone who had one drink too many last night, danced one song over his limit and woken up too early to deal with such distressing news. We sat in the living room watching Emily sleep, whispering and plotting the demise of one Joe Steiner. We envisioned a slow painful imaginary death. Matt made me go over every detail of the attack, twisting and smacking an innocent magazine the whole time.

Matt went to the hospital to be with his sister, and he called and told us she was doing okay, considering. The main thing was that she was conscious. We drank a pot of coffee and had leftovers from the casserole Ronnie had made the night before.

We sat around the living room, consoled each other and hugged and cried it out. That gave me the strength and encouragement to finally stop shaking and unclench my jaw. I dozed on and off, exhaustion and a second painkiller finally taking over.

Linda and Ronnie's kids woke up and they carefully explained that Emily'd had a rough night and needed some extra sleep. Could Cameron take her brothers and play until Emily woke up? Cameron puffed up her big sister chest and explained to the boys that she was in charge, let's go to the basement to watch some cartoons! All morning, the kids were little angels, staying in the basement, playing and hanging out. But, every once in a while, Cameron would sneak back upstairs to peek in on Emily, still fast asleep on the couch. One of us would see her and smile, causing Cameron to turn and run back downstairs.

When Emily finally woke up, around noon, I called Matt and he came back over with Marti. Matt held her in his arms promising her he would stay with her for now. Emily cried again, recalling every moment of the assault. We rallied around her and told her how brave she was. I don't think she believed me when I told her *she* was the reason her mom and I hadn't been hurt any more than we had been. Ronnie fed Emily, and Matt, Marti, Emily and I headed out to visit Corin.

The hospital had put her in a private room. The police officer at the door checked all our IDs and let us in. It was warm and dark in there and Corin looked tiny surrounded by all the equipment and monitors. Emily was small enough to lie beside Corin. Matt and I delegated ourselves to the far corners at the foot of her bed, Marti leaning against the back wall.

I tried not to make a sound when I saw Corin but I'm pretty sure I inhaled sharply. Corin's right eye was completely shut, her left a mere slit. She was black and blue and purple on her face, upper arms and part of her neck. Her left arm had a temporary light cast. She whispered that the break would need surgery. She looked defeated and drained, bruised and battered, afraid and very small.

"Don't worry about a thing, baby sister," Matt's voice trembled slightly. "Devan and I will take care of you and Emily. He won't hurt you again. I promise you that. I should have been there for you. I knew, deep down inside, something bad would happen to you because of him. Ever since he hit you the first time, I knew he would do it again. I guess I just thought if I didn't think about it, it wouldn't happen."

"Don't put Devan on the spot like that, Matt. She shouldn't get involved in my problems. I can handle this myself." I can only assume Corin tried to give Matt a look of warning but it came across as a little sad and desperate.

"Of course I'm involved in this, Corin. I care about you and Emily and don't want you to get hurt anymore than you already have. And Steiner just *made* me involved in this." I stood up and started pacing in the little room, wincing just a little at the pain in my side. "The police will find Steiner and lock him up. But until that time we'll work on keeping the two of you safe. We can't go back to the house."

"Yes. I hate that but okay."

"What about a weapon? Do either of you have a weapon?" Both Corin and Matt shook their heads. "Maybe we should look into getting a gun for Corin. What do you think?"

"I can't have one around Emily," Corin said, looking at her daughter.

"Why don't we talk with Sam before we do anything rash?" Marti's voice came floating up from the back of the room. "I think some self-defense training would do us all some good."

Matt suggested, "I'm all for it. Let's get a bazooka for the SOB!"

"I'm scared," Emily said, forcing us to look at her, her eyes wide with fright, bringing us back to the here and now.

"I'm sorry, Em! I didn't mean that. I forget you're only eleven sometimes. You seem much older," Matt said with a hint of embarrassment.

"We'll be okay, Emily baby. I promise." And then Corin smiled. A slow movement of her face but the first real smile I had seen on her since we met. Emily hugged her mother tightly which undoubtedly hurt Corin's bruised body but Corin seemed happy for her daughter's touch.

Sam came into the room, hugged everyone and ended up by the side of Corin's bed. "How are you feeling right now, Corin?"

"I'm sore and tired. I just want to fall asleep and pretend this never happened."

"Well, the detectives are here and *they* won't pretend this never happened. They want to know why Steiner picked now to attack you. Do you feel up to talking with them or should I tell them to come back after you've slept a while?"

"They can come in now. I don't know what to tell them. I don't know why he did this. He wasn't like this when I first met him."

"Something must have set him off. Was he drunk? High? He hit you once several months ago and then nothing. Have you talked with him lately?"

"Yes I did, come to think of it. He called a few days ago and was very upset about his stuff being out in the garage and his key not working. When you had me change the locks I completely forgot about the garage. I changed that lock a couple of weeks ago and Joe was not happy about it. He went on and on about not having access to his stuff and about the…umm…woman living in his garage." Corin turned her bloody and bruised eyes on me. "Sorry, Devan."

"Don't be. It's okay," I said. "I'm sure he had more colorful word choices than that."

"Yes, he did," Corin said.

"Let me go talk with the detectives," Sam said, turning to go.

"Wait, Sam. Why can't I just talk with you and you can talk with the detectives?"

"It doesn't work like that, honey. They'll need to talk with you in person." Sam walked back to the far side of her bed and kneeled down to talk with her. "Corin, I'll be right here for you if you need me. I'm not going anywhere. Matt has your phone and I've programmed all my numbers into it in case you need me. I'm not going anywhere until you ask me to leave. Okay?"

"Okay. Thanks, Sam." She put her good hand on Sam's forearm and they stayed like that for a moment.

"I'm just going outside the door to talk with the detectives." Corin followed her with her good eye.

When the detectives and Sam came in, I dragged Matt and Marti out into the hallway to plot our strategy. Matt decided Emily would stay with him and Corin would join them when she was able. Everyone would do what they could to help Matt whether that be cooking, cleaning or running errands. We were all on edge, exhausted, stunned by the brutality, afraid this was only the beginning.

CHAPTER THIRTY-ONE

The next morning, when I called to check on Emily, I told Matt I would cancel going to Maui but he talked me out of it. He said something about how crazy I would be if I gave up the opportunity, and it wasn't happening for eight weeks. He did briefly try and talk me into letting him go instead but when that angle didn't work, went back to what a waste it would be if I didn't grab this by the balls (his words) and ride it for all it was worth. I had to agree with him, having given up the idea I was Wonder Woman before I hit my midtwenties, noticing how people generally did okay without me around. It would be *considerate* if someone fell apart without me but that didn't seem to be the case. Damn. I'd just have to go to Maui with Alex.

Lori came over to Linda and Ronnie's for dinner one night about a week after the attack. I had helped Ronnie make our dinner of spaghetti and meatballs and was learning a lot about cooking from her. Since I was spending so much time with Linda and Ronnie we were becoming very good friends. Of course, I helped around the house and paid for groceries and rent, and that seemed to actually help them out a little. Corin kindly waived the rent on my apartment since I was too afraid to live there with Steiner on the loose.

Linda borrowed a spare bed from a friend and we took it into the basement after bringing the Ping-Pong table outside. Sam took me to my apartment and I packed a couple of bags of clothes and my toiletries. I was really hoping this would be a temporary living situation since it stayed pretty cold downstairs.

"I can't believe that asshole Joe sent her to the hospital again!" Lori said.

"He was trying to kill her. I could see it in his eyes," I said.

"Do we have any word on him? Do they have any leads on where he is?" Ronnie asked.

"No. I saw Sam the other day and she said they have no idea where he is. They're watching his mom's house because that's where he'll likely go if he needs something, but other than that..." Linda said.

"His mom is a piece of work too. Has anyone met her?" Ronnie asked. We all said no as we dished up our food. "I was at the Ace Hardware store about a year ago and heard some yelling. When I came around the corner I realized it was Matt and a woman I'd seen around but didn't know. I stood and watched them yell at each other for a few minutes until I got Matt's attention. After she left in a huff and after Matt cooled off for a minute, he said that was Joe's mom.

"She was awful. She said some horrible things about Corin. Mostly how she wasn't good enough for her angel Joe and she was glad when he dumped Corin. Either she was delusional or Joe told her all kinds of untrue things. I've never seen Matt so angry. Totally out of character for him."

With a mouth full of meatball I said, "I hope they find him soon. I would love for our lives to go back to something resembling normal."

"You could come stay with me, Devan, if Linda and Ronnie are tired of you," Lori offered.

"Don't you dare take away my new best friend," said Ronnie. "She helps me with the kids, with cleaning and is really becoming a great cook."

"Thank you, Ronnie. Not true but I do like to help with the chores."

"Where are the kids?" Lori asked.

"They're next door," Linda said. "Should I be worried here, Ron? Are you replacing me?"

"No. I just appreciate the fact Devan is helping me more than I realized possible. I wasn't expecting any help at all and I'm thrilled she cares enough to vacuum and dust."

"I could vacuum and dust," Linda said. She had stopped eating and was looking at Ronnie with big eyes.

"You could but you don't."

The air became thick and harder to breath. I was concentrating so hard on eating my dinner, Lori startled me by saying, "Sorry, I just thought you two might want a little more privacy. Just know I have a spare bedroom, Devan."

"We definitely don't need any *privacy* now, do we Linda?"

"Can we just enjoy this delicious meal and save our difficulties for the privacy of our bedroom, please, Ronnie?"

"Of course. Not like we do anything else in there."

To Linda's credit she didn't say anything else. As a matter of fact, none of us said anything after that. We finished eating and cleaned up the kitchen. Lori and I took our wine out to the front porch to talk and give Linda and Ronnie some space.

"Seriously, if you want to come stay with me just let me know, okay?" Lori said as she sat on the bench. I sat next to her and she placed her free hand on my leg.

"I will if Ronnie or Linda ask me to but I'm enjoying spending time with them. They are really great people. Ronnie was a little intense when I first met her but she's really wonderful when you get to know her. And Linda's a riot."

"I didn't realize how bad things were between them."

"It's not normally like this. I think they need to work on communication because they're usually pleasant to each other. Just every once in a while the simmering pot boils over."

"Just know I'm here for you." She looked at me and smiled, rubbing my thigh. "I'm here for you for whatever you need."

"Thank you. That's nice to know. I wanted to talk with you about Thanksgiving." I had been hemming and hawing about telling her then I realized I had to tell her. I couldn't just leave town and not say why. That just seemed wrong. I just didn't want her to get the wrong idea about my trip with Alex. Just a couple of friends going to a tropical island to relax. Hmmm…I should call Alex and see what she's doing.

"Yes?" I must have been thinking a little too hard because Lori was looking at me the way Ronnie sometimes looked at the kids. Like please tell me because I'm hanging here and it appears you have forgotten me. "You really do talk with yourself don't you?"

"Sorry yes. It's getting worse I think. Anyhoo…I'm going to Maui with Alex for Thanksgiving." Sometimes I just have to say things bluntly. I'd have to work on that.

"Really?" Lori leaned back on the bench and took her hand off my thigh. "With Alex?"

"Yup just two friends going on vacation. Nothing more than that." Absolutely nothing more than that.

"Hmmm. I don't know what to say. I was really hoping you and I had something special between us."

"No! I mean yes! We do have something special." I turned putting my leg on the bench between us and looked into her eyes. "Alex had an extra ticket and invited me spur of the moment because Cleo couldn't go with her leg the way it is."

"Okay."

"There is nothing going on between Alex and me, I swear."

She looked at me for a long minute then said, "Good because it bothers me thinking you're seeing someone else."

Oh crap. I looked away from Lori and into my beer.

"You're not seeing anyone else are you Devan?"

"Well…"

"Who are you seeing?"

"I've been casually dating the woman I met at Ladies' Night Out."

"Kelly? You're seeing Kelly Carpenter?"

"Yes, just casually." Did I really have to tell the truth all the time?

Lori drained her beer and said, "I feel a little crowded here." She stood up and walked into the house to recycle her bottle and get her jacket.

When she came back out I said, "You don't have to go."

"Yes, I think I do. Why don't you call me if you cross off any names from your little black book." And with that she was gone. I sat there for several minutes and wondered if I could have done anything differently to change that outcome. Probably.

* * *

After the initial shock of the attack wore off and Emily came to realize her mom would be okay, she relaxed and settled back into school and her new life of visiting mom and playing with Linda and Ronnie's kids. When not in school, Cameron and Emily spent most of their time together rolling their eyes and giggling, exasperated over the antics of the two young, rambunctious boys.

After surgery on her arm, Corin was allowed to leave the hospital and join Emily and Matt at his place. The plan was that she'd stay there until her arm had healed completely, and hopefully by then, Joe would have been apprehended.

After I hadn't been to the gym for a week Alex called, wondering where I was. She had been busy with work and didn't realize what had happened. She was mad no one called her and went over to visit with Corin during her lunch break. She came by Linda and Ronnie's after work and checked to make sure I was okay, too. I told her I was fine—I hadn't been beaten unconscious by a maniac. Alex started calling me frequently asking how I was doing. She also came by to have a beer with me most nights. I told Alex she would be sick of me by the time we left for Maui but she just laughed it off saying that wasn't possible.

Matt was thoughtful enough to clean up Corin's bedroom in preparation for her eventual return to her place. He tried to launder the sheets, thought better of it and bought her new ones. He had the window locks replaced, arranged for the alarm company to install an alarm and extended the security system to my apartment. We all had high hopes the police would catch Steiner quickly so Corin could relax, just a little, and regain her life.

Despite budget constraints the police did the best they could helping with drive-bys and courtesy calls. Sam did even more. She worked nights and spent all her breaks parked in front of Matt's house, watching and waiting. She came over a couple of times that first week, with her police uniform, patrol car and Glock nine millimeter, bringing a sense of security to Corin. Sam also enrolled us all in self-defense classes with Corin promising to take hers at a later date.

A seemingly constant stream of Matt and Corin's friends came over to Matt's bringing casseroles, books, laughter and healing over those eight weeks. When Corin felt well enough to travel, we brought her and Emily over to Linda and Ronnie's so the kids could play. We sang karaoke, which the kids loved almost as much as the adults, and played games outside: badminton, soccer, flag football and softball. We almost forgot about the danger lurking in the dark corners, almost let our guard down. But every time a phone rang we all tensed up just a little. An unusual noise outside would cause the adults in the room to get up and quietly do a perimeter search.

About two weeks after the attack Kelly called me one night, apologizing about standing me up. I was still angry and hurt when we talked and at first I didn't want to make any plans at all but we finally decided to meet for coffee at the Nutt House after school the next day.

"I can't tell you how sorry I am Devan. I got wrapped up at work and forgot to call you." We had settled into a back booth with our coffee to talk.

"I don't understand you Kelly. One minute you tell me how much you care for me the next I don't hear from you in two weeks."

"I know. I'm sorry. It's one of my weaknesses. I tend to get all wrapped up in a new adventure and forget to breathe." She took one of hands and kissed it. "Please forgive me. Maybe next time you can come to San Francisco with me."

"I have to work, Kelly." I was still mad but my angry mask was cracking. Being near her warmed my cold insides. "What are you doing in San Fran?"

"I'm working with Bruce, my best friend from high school. We're creating software which caters to healthcare companies. We think there's a huge hole in the supply chain and we plan on plugging that hole."

"Sounds great."

"Yeah, it will be." She slid closer to me and said, "What are you doing for Thanksgiving? Maybe you could come down with me and I can show you how thankful I am for you?"

Oh crap. I really need to work on my planning skills. How am I caught off guard so much? "I can't, I'm sorry. I have other plans."

"Okay. Are you finally going up to see your parents?" Damn! Now I have to call my parents too. Should I tell her the truth or make up a little white lie? She won't even notice I'm gone since she can't see beyond her new enterprise. Maybe I'll just make up a little lie. Nothing's going to happen with Alex so why even worry Kelly with that information. And after Lori's reaction there's nothing wrong with glossing over a few minor facts.

"No, I'm just hanging out with friends for the holiday." I guess that's not really a boldfaced lie. I *am* hanging out with a friend (Alex).

"I'd love it if you could join me. The city of love."

"How long will you be down in California?"

"I'm leaving next week and I'll be down there until at least the beginning of December."

"Why so long?"

"If we want to go live in the spring we have to make a big push now to get it up and running. We'll save the debugging for the winter. I might have to stay longer if things don't go well."

"Oh, well, I'll think about coming down in December if you're still there."

"Don't worry about a ticket. I'll use points to bring you down."

"Then I'll seriously think about it."

"That would be wonderful, Devan."

"Yes, that would be fun."

CHAPTER THIRTY-TWO

When the time came for me to leave for Maui, I was ready to get away from waiting for the proverbial other shoe to fall, and just relax. I felt bad for Corin. She couldn't fly away and feel safe like I could, couldn't leave everything behind and put an ocean between her and her dangerous ex-husband.

Alex came early in the morning to drive us to the airport where we waited in line with all the other happy travelers leaving town. We were herded onto the airplane and settled in for the five-hour flight. I was still a little tense during the flight, worried about Corin and Emily, and didn't start relaxing until the captain started the descent. It took breaking beneath the clouds, circling around the island of Maui preparing to land, for a small smile to spread across my face.

I'd heard how wonderful Hawaii was, how beautiful and tropical and lush. But I wasn't prepared for how amazing it really was. The skies were clear and blue and the air had a deep, rich quality. Alex's cousin Kai picked us up at the airport. He was a large man, tall and broad-shouldered. A native Hawaiian, Kai had the dark tan skin that I could only dream about. Alex had told me on the plane that after a week on Maui she would be as dark as the locals. I told her after a week on Maui I would be a burnt red woman who would stick out like a sore thumb.

"Where is everyone?" Alex asked Kai after he had put her down.

"They're waiting for you at *hale Makuahine*. They couldn't all fit in the car and too many arguments." He smiled, saw the confusion on my face and said, "They're waiting at my mom's, Kukona's, house."

"Oh, thanks. I'll have to learn a little Hawaiian."

"Well, if we could convince Alex and Cleo to move back to Maui, you could move here too! Really get to know our language and culture." With the bright blue sky framing Kai he made a compelling argument.

"If it were only that easy."

"Give me a couple of years cousin, I'm working on it," Alex said while pulling our suitcases off the belt. "You could help, Kai. Devan's bags are really heavy."

"Hey! They're not that heavy," I protested.

"From the looks of *your* arms, Alex, you don't need any help," Kai said.

Maui's airport was in Kahului, and Kai's house-sitting job was a little up the coast near the town of Waiehu. The drive was filled with such staggering views all I could say was "Ooooh" and "Aaaah" from the backseat of Kai's Mustang convertible. The house was impressive as well...the perfectly manicured landscaping matched by the dream house to beat all other dream houses. Kai led us to our rooms, which were side by side, attached by a Jack and Jill bathroom.

My room was large and breezy with a view of the beach and further out, the Pacific. The room alone was larger than my little apartment in Vancouver, with floor-to-ceiling windows, a spacious patio I now know is called a lanai and one very large king-size bed. I wandered over to Alex's room and found her standing by her large window gazing longingly out at the sea. I stood by her, the two of us just looking at the view until Alex suggested we go to the kitchen to talk with Kai.

"Come on, you two," Kai said as we entered the kitchen, "let's go. Mom just called and everyone's there waiting for us."

On the drive over to Kukona's house on the western edge of Kahului, Kai said, "I hope you two don't mind but I was kind of hoping you would watch the house while my girlfriend and I went over to the Big Island for a couple of days. I don't mean to be rude. I know you just got here but her family is having a big reunion and we have to go."

"Only if you come visit us in Vancouver over the summer," Alex said.

"Done," Kai said, patting Alex on the shoulder.

* * *

We pulled up to Alex's aunt's place. The colorful little house couldn't have been more than twelve hundred square feet and it was packed with people of all shapes and sizes. When Alex's family saw us pull up, a collective gasp went through the crowd and everyone ran down and surrounded the car. Alex turned around to talk with me.

"Don't worry, nobody bites. I'll try and introduce everyone but some of the new family members, the ones who married in, those I'm a little shaky on."

"Okay."

"Don't worry I'll help you with names, Alex," Kai said.

"Thanks, *Hoahānau*."

After everyone and I mean *everyone*, hugged Alex, Kukona walked up to me, placed her hands on my face and said, "*Lani kea wahine*." Um, thank you? Everyone laughed and cheered after Kukona's exclamation and even Alex was smiling from ear to ear, so I assumed it was a good thing so I expressed my thanks out loud.

"Welcome to my home, Devan. It is so nice to meet you," Kukona said, letting go of my face.

"Thank you, Kukona. I'm sure you'd rather see Cleo but I'm very happy to be here."

"We would love to see Cleo but we are grateful she is okay now. We will see her soon, I'm sure. My sister comes over frequently. Maybe she'll bring Cleo with her next time." She put her arm through mine and walked with me up to the house. "We are very happy to meet you. Alex has never brought one of her friends here. You must be very special to her."

"Oh thank you." I didn't feel the need to explain Alex's and my relationship to her. Alex could do that in time.

Throughout the night, Alex introduced me to everyone in the house: numerous aunts and uncles, nieces and nephews, boyfriends and girlfriends and various friends and neighbors. Everyone had brought something to eat or drink and we nibbled all night. Kukona made mai tais for everyone and they quickly became my favorite drink. Everyone wanted to talk with Alex, get caught up with her life, but she managed to stay by my side. I think she was a little concerned I'd be overwhelmed by all the attention but I was having a great time. It was unlike anything I had ever experienced and, instead of overwhelming me, Alex's family intrigued me.

"Are you okay?" Alex asked me as she filled my drink up again.

"Yes, I'm fine. Don't worry about me. Everyone is so accommodating. I couldn't be happier."

"Good. I was a little worried it would be too much."

"No. I love being here." I laid my hand on Alex's arm to emphasize how much I was enjoying myself.

"Oh...kay," Alex said. "Does that mean it would be okay if I grab a ukulele and joined Uncle Puhi?"

"Oh crap. Really?" I said to Alex's back. I had a roommate in college who insisted the ukulele was the best instrument...ever! And played it badly, loudly and at the most inopportune times. Alex, on the other hand, could really play. I sat with her family feeling comfortable and safe, and listened to Alex and her uncle.

Midway through the concert, with Alex calling for requests, I migrated over to Kukona, who was in the kitchen preparing another chicken.

"Hi honey. Do you need another mai tai? Some more food?" As she asked me she was reaching for the rum.

"No, I'm fine. Thank you. What a wonderful childhood Alex and Cleo must have had here on the island."

"Oh, Alex and Cleo, those two! They were two of the same. They lived in the water. You couldn't get them off those surfboards. Such little girls and such big boards!" Kukona laughed at the memories. "It was hard when they left, very hard, but Frank had to go."

"That must have been hard on the girls too." I leaned back on the counter, getting comfortable.

"Yes. They didn't want to go. But Portland is special too in a different way. The girls adjusted. Cleo more than Alex. Alex always talked about moving back when she was old enough to live on her own. She never did but she still talks about moving back."

"I think the gym ties her to the Portland area but I can see her moving back. She looks incredibly happy to be home." I glanced over at Alex laughing with her uncle, amazed at how relaxed and happy she seemed. She wore a smile that inspired me to smile as well. I looked back at Kukona who was also smiling.

"Yes. It's a very happy place, Maui. I can see you living here too, one day soon."

I didn't know what to say. No sense arguing about something like that. I looked out the back window and notice a potted plant on the lanai. "Is that a hydrangea? I'm surprised they grow out here."

"Yes. The first time I traveled to Portland, I fell in love with the big beautiful shrubs Pua called hydrangeas. I brought one back and it immediately died after I planted it in the garden. They only grow in pots here and don't last very long but I just love them. Alex and Cleo send one to me every year so I can enjoy them while they last."

She turned back to the chicken and I looked back at Alex who had settled her gaze on me. She waved me over and I went to her and sat on the floor next to her chair, watching her strum the ukulele, swept away on the current of the room.

After Alex and I had eaten all we could eat and drank all we could drink, we decided it was time to go. Alex's family tried to convince us to stay but it felt much later than what the clock said. Since Maui is three hours behind Vancouver, it really *was* later to our bodies. We hugged everyone and said goodnight.

Kai drove us back to the house and walked us around showing us the important things like remote control procedures, alarm sequences and cleaning supplies.

"Can you believe we woke up in Vancouver this morning and here we are sitting in Maui?" Alex asked me after Kai had left us alone sitting on the lanai off the living room.

"I can't quite wrap my mind around it but the drinks help. It's so beautiful. Can we move here?"

"Whoa! Slow down, Devan. Now you're asking me to move in with you. Let's just get through the next few days okay?" It was obvious she was proud of her wit.

"You know what I mean. Let's not go back. Don't make me go back. I can't imagine having anyone attack me here. I feel safe, which I haven't for some time." I was certain I couldn't go back to my normal life. The breeze coming off the Pacific was perfect, just warm enough to let you know you were on a tropical island but cool enough to be relaxing.

"Okay, we'll stay. We can get jobs and sleep on the beach. I'm all for it."

"That sounds wonderful," I said. "But bed first. I'm so tired."

"Whoa! Slow down, filly."

"Stop it. Don't go there," I warned. "Good night, Alex."

"Good night, Devan. Sleep well," she chuckled. She got up from her chair and walked to the open sliding glass door.

"Hey, Alex."

"Yes?" She turned back toward me.

"What did your aunt say to me when she had my face in her hands?" I asked.

"She called you a heavenly white woman," Alex replied and stepped through into the house.

CHAPTER THIRTY-THREE

I slept long and deeply, waking up before the dawn. I put on my new uniform: a bathing suit, which looked better on me after all the hard work at the gym, shirt, shorts and sandals and went down to make coffee. Alex had beaten me to it and was out on the lanai breathing in the fresh sea breeze. She had her back to me and, as I lingered by the couch, I watched her drink her coffee. She wore her bathing suit, a small tank top and shorts, and I could see a lizard tattoo on her back, near her right shoulder. It was black, about six inches long and gave her an air of the exotic. She turned to look at me and smiled.

"Good morning, sleepyhead. What are you smiling about?"

"Nothing. I'm just a dork."

She turned back to the ocean breeze and I thought I heard her say, "That is *so* true," but I couldn't be sure. I got a cup of coffee and joined her. As I watched the sun rise, standing on a lanai in Maui, I had the strongest urge to run down the street yelling at the top of my lungs. I held it in though.

"Hey, let's go for a walk, can we?"

"Sure. Whatever you want," Alex said. After eating some fresh pineapple, we wound down to the beach carrying our sandals, letting our toes enjoy the warm golden sand. The smells of the restaurants sparked a fire in my stomach.

I asked, "Can we stop and get something to eat?"

"What the pineapple didn't fill you up?"

"No. Actually, it just made my stomach angry," I said. We stopped by a little bistro a block or so off the beach, ordering Portuguese sausage, eggs and rice. We ate at a leisurely pace in no hurry to get anywhere or do anything. We talked about growing up and growing older.

"So tell me, Devan. Where do you see yourself in ten years?"

"Oh, Alex. Don't ask such hard questions. It feels like a job interview."

"Seriously. What do you see yourself doing?"

"I don't know. I haven't really thought about it. If you had asked me that question a year ago I wouldn't have said get dumped, get fired and move to Vancouver, Washington." I pushed my plate away and leaned back in the chair, a cup of coffee in my hands. "I don't know what's going to happen and I don't know if I want to predict…my life probably will take a detour if I say anything out loud." I took a sip and asked Alex, "What about you? Where do you see yourself ten years from now?"

"I see myself married to an incredibly beautiful woman, living with her in my little house, having a dog or two, maybe even a cat, growing my business into the corporate fitness program side and expanding Finesse all over town and down into Portland with at least twenty stores." Alex stated this all matter-of-factly.

"Oh, so you haven't thought about it either?"

"I think about it all the time. I've told my family here, many times, I would love to move back and live on the island but I can't see that happening yet. I can, ultimately, see me and my wife owning a little shack on the beach where we can come any time we can get away."

Not what I was expecting from Alex. That doesn't sound anything like the woman I've been getting to know, the woman who can't commit. I'm not sure she can live up to such lofty goals.

Since she brought it up, what do I want out of life? Do I want to get married? I do want to be loved, that is the truth, but do I need to be married to do that?

"Nice. I can't think about that right now though. Maybe later."

"Are you done eating? We should go for a swim." Alex placed her napkin on the table and got up. She reached her hand over to help me up. I took it and allowed myself to be carried away into the brilliant blue sky.

We headed north on Highway 30 in Kai's car toward Napili, stopping at one of the numerous pullouts along the way, watching the locals swimming and playing in the water below. The water was so clear and blue, Alex spotted a stingray gliding effortlessly through the water. If Alex hadn't convinced me the next pullout would be just as breathtaking, I probably wouldn't have got back in the Mustang.

We drove up and parked near DT Fleming Beach Park, walking in with our borrowed snorkeling gear for an afternoon of floating with sea creatures. I had to stop and catch my breath midstream when Alex took off her tank top. She was wearing a small rainbow striped bikini with board shorts that showed off her perfect physique. She looked amazing: strong and feminine at the same time. She didn't seem to notice me looking at her, which was a good thing because I didn't want to hear about it.

The water was warm and inviting. We swam in the gentle waters of the bay until dusk. Alex tried to talk me into staying in the water but I convinced her sharks could come by and eat me at any moment in the dark. I had seen the movies. She just laughed at me, shaking her head at my childish notions, while looking at me with a tenderness that made my heart feel strange. What was going on with this maddening woman?

We had drinks on the beach in one of the numerous restaurants, and watched the sun go down, hypnotic in its kaleidoscope of reds. It was a perfect ending to my first full day on the Islands, filling me with a joy I'd never felt before.

"You look very happy, Devan."

"Oh, you have *no* idea," I said and she didn't. I felt at peace, sitting with a view of the water, with a good friend, without a worry in the world.

"Have you talked with Corin or Matt?"

"No. Oops, I guess I should do that now before it gets too late." So much for ignorant bliss. As I expected, nobody fell apart when I left. They seemed to be carrying on just fine without me.

"Oh, that reminds me. How is Cleo doing?"

"Much better since she went home. She's even doing a little work from the house. She's been going to physical therapy for five weeks now and she's making real progress. Her ribs still hurt but she seems to be on the mend. Her leg will take a long time to heal, I'm afraid. I think it's too soon for her to be doing anything work-related but she doesn't listen to me, or anyone for that matter. She wanted me to tell you hello and to not put up with any of my BS. Next time you see her will you tell her I did as I was told?"

"She's so thoughtful. I'll tell her."

"Thanks. I don't know why she gives me so much grief," Alex said.

"I think *I* do."

"It's really hard being me."

"Well, I know it's hard to be *with* you. Maybe you won't be so annoying if I spend more time with you," I said with a smile to soften my words.

"I doubt it will help but you can give it a try. I've heard it before: you just want to love me but I'm so damned annoying."

"Yeah. Something like that."

After unpacking our things and hanging up our suits to dry, we headed over to Kukona's house. There weren't as many people the second night, none of the neighbors and friends.

"Ah, Devan! So nice to see you again. I was hoping you two would come by and see us," Kukona said.

"Why thank you. You're so charming. We spent the day swimming and lying in the sun."

"Yes, I can see that. You might want to buy some aloe for the pain," Kukona said, bringing me under the light to get a better look at me.

"Don't worry. It's perfectly normal. The burn looks worse than it really is," I said, a red woman surrounded by strikingly tan people.

"Really? Because it looks pretty bad," Alex said with just a hint of kindness.

We ate dinner on the lanai, surrounded by the tropical plants Kukona loved to grow. The pork was delicious, the macaroni salad a creamy delight and I couldn't get enough of the fresh pineapple. It just seemed to taste different on the island. Various family members told me long, funny stories about Alex and Cleo when they were young. Alex spent the rest of the evening saying, "That's not true," and "Hey! I never did that! That was totally Cleo."

By eight o'clock, I could barely keep my eyes open and Alex took pity on me telling everyone how tired she was and that we really had to go. Kukona wanted us to stay over but we begged off telling her all our things were at the house. Plus, we were supposed to be minding it.

We drove in silence up to the house and I fell asleep somewhere along the way. I awakened to Alex trying to pick me up out of the car, one of her arms behind my head and the other under my knees. Actually, I think I woke up when she grunted.

"What are you doing?"

"Well, I was trying not to wake you. You looked so peaceful sleeping there so I tried to pick you up but you're heavier than you look."

"Oh, thanks for that. Not only did you wake me up but you called me a fat ass."

"You do not have a fat ass. You just have more muscle mass than I was expecting. Absolutely nothing wrong with your ass, trust me," she said with a smile.

I walked in under my own power, we said our good nights and got ready for bed. The time change really took the partying out of me, which is not saying much but it felt much later than the clock said. I heard a soft knock on the door and went to answer it. Alex was standing there with bottles of water. She didn't wear much to bed but I was grateful for what little she was wearing, looking fit, tanned and healthy in her boxers and tank top.

"You've had a lot of sun, and I don't want you to dehydrate. If you need anything I'll be right through the bathroom okay?" she said as she pointed to the bathroom door.

"Thanks. I'll be fine, Alex. Go to bed. Quit bugging me. You were over there last night too."

CHAPTER THIRTY-FOUR

Still affected by jetlag, we rose bright and early the next morning, and armed with coffee, planned our day. Life was full of hard choices on Maui. Should we do the Road to Hana today or tomorrow? Should we go to the beach and let Alex watch me take surfing lessons, stand up paddleboard lessons or should we snorkel? Or should we chuck it all and park ourselves at the beach?

"It's your choice, Alex. I've never been here and I want to do everything. What do you want to do today?" I didn't care what we did or where we went.

"The Road to Hana. We're up early enough to make the drive down and back today."

"Okay."

"Let's load up on supplies on the way out," Alex said, taking charge. "Wear your swimsuit. There are a few waterfalls we can hit along the way and I have a reservation at the Fish House for dinner. That's the restaurant Cleo and I go to every year. They have the best Macadamia Nut Crusted Stuffed Mahimahi on the island."

We packed up, jumped in Kai's Mustang and headed out before the sun. We passed Hookipa Beach Park and I was surprised by the number of people already there. The parking lot was packed. Alex told me that the surfing on Maui was pretty good overall, but Hookipa Beach was the best surfing spot on Maui, period. In the early mornings the conditions were perfect. When the trade winds picked up after noon, the windsurfers came out to play. Alex assured me we could stop by in the afternoon to watch them as the restaurant was only a couple of minutes from the beach.

Along our long, windy trip, we saw eucalyptus trees, mountain apple trees (with their bright red flowers), forests of bamboo, hibiscus and the kukui nut tree (also known as the candlenut), Hawaii's State Tree.

"I have a strong tie to the kukui nut tree," Alex said.

"Really? How so? Is it because you're a bit of a nut yourself?"

"Well, kind of. About five years ago, I had the lizard put on my back. I had it done here on Maui and the artist used ink derived from the kukui nut."

"Yes, that would explain a lot."

Maui was lush and tropical, bright and beautiful. Our first chance to hike came on the Waikamoi Forest Ridge Trail, a short family-friendly loop which climbed up into the eucalyptus trees. It was a short, up-and-down trail with views of the ocean in the distance. We arrived at the trailhead alone but when we returned the small parking lot was filled with cars. Fortunately, because of our early start it seemed we were slightly ahead of the crowd.

Our next walk was at the serene Ke'anae Arboretum, a man-made tropical rainforest with placards explaining the multitude of plants introduced on Maui. We strolled down a paved walkway amongst monkey pod trees, red, white and torch ginger, fields of taro plants and our personal favorite, the rainbow eucalyptus trees. According to the placard, when the tree was wet a rainbow of colors would appear on the bark.

The closer we got to Hana, the closer to perfect the weather became. When we pulled into the tiny village of Hana the sky was clear and the temperature a pleasant seventy-two degrees with a cool breeze. It was cooler and drier on that part of the island and, on a clear day, Hana residents can see a glimpse of the Big Island of Hawaii from their homes.

We reluctantly headed back, not wanting to leave but we didn't want to make the drive to Kahului in the dark. It was terror inducing enough during the day. It was much quicker on the return trip. We had to hurry in order to make it in time for our dinner reservations at the Fish House. I think we both wished we had worn something a little less casual but were too hungry to really care that much.

The valets parked the car for us and the hostess guided us past the expansive restaurant on our left and the pristine beachfront on the right, to the second hostess stand in the back. We were seated in the open-air restaurant, right in the front, with a great view of the ocean.

"This is amazing. When did you have to make these reservations?"

Alex responded, "I made them a few months ago. Cleo and I just love it here. It's a wonderful view isn't it?"

"Yes. I'm sorry you had to settle for me instead."

"I'm not settling. I can't think of anyone else I would rather be with."

How should I respond to that? I had spent the day with Alex, mostly sitting beside her in the car, laughing. We swam together, huddled together for warmth, experienced the at times nauseating drive to Hana together and witnessed one beautiful sight after the other together. I couldn't think of anyone else either. "Thank you, Alex. I love being with you too." Too much?

We ate one of the best meals I have ever had the pleasure of putting in my mouth. We both ordered the mahimahi and we both cleaned our plates. The mai tais were strong and delicious, expensive but worth every penny. We sat at our table, with the food and drink just another happy memory, and watched the sun set over the private beach. It was perfect, picturesque and unforgettable. I kept these feelings to myself as we made our way back to the house. I was afraid I'd said too much to Alex about how much I loved being with her. I didn't want to send her the wrong idea. I couldn't see our new relationship going anywhere beyond friendly. Could I? As we walked through the front door, Alex held my hand, not letting go until we had reached the living room.

She didn't say anything when we entered the house, pulling me toward her when we had passed through the door, kissing me gently. She caught me off guard, so I kissed her back. I couldn't help it. Kissing her seemed like the right thing to do. We kissed, our hands running over each other's bodies, until there was no air left between us, until I felt I couldn't take it anymore, until my ringing phone forced me to pull away. I was out of breath, lost in Alex, when I realized it was Matt calling. Oh no. Not again. Please tell me good news Matt.

"Matt! What's wrong? Is everyone okay?" I was afraid of his response.

"Whoa! Everything's okay. We're all fine. I just wanted to see how you two were doing. Did I interrupt something? You seem a little out of breath." He was grinning when he said that last part. I could hear it in his voice.

"Don't be ridiculous. I had to run for the phone." Lying was becoming a little too easy. "How's Corin doing?"

"She's doing just fine. She even had a little sip of my wine but don't tell the doctors!" *Matt* had obviously had more than a little sip of wine.

"Good. I was worried about you guys. What time is it?"

"So stop worrying and enjoy yourself. It's pretty late. We're having a little party here at L and R's. We'll raise a glass for you and Alex. You girls be good. Don't do anything I wouldn't do."

"That leaves me wide open then doesn't it? Thanks, Matt, and say hi to everyone for us."

"Everyone okay?" Alex asked.

"Yeah. Everyone is doing just fine."

I looked up into Alex's eyes and saw her desire was still there. But for me the spell had been broken. I needed to get a little space between us before I did something stupid. I stepped back from her, intent on rearranging the various knickknacks on the shelves. I was afraid to turn around and face her, afraid of what I would see in her eyes, afraid of what my response would be. Alex dispelled my fears by turning me around to face her, whether I wanted to or not.

"Are you okay?" I saw the concern in her eyes.

"Yes, I'm fine. I just need to think about that kiss for a while. I'm not sure what this means. I'm not Cathy. I can't just have sex with you and not have it mean anything." Although, parts of me really wanted to, I must admit.

"I know you're not Cathy. Cathy and I are just friends who happen to enjoy having sex together. I don't want to be your *friend*."

My crossed arms and frown seemed to get my feelings across sufficiently.

"Not in that sense! Listen, from the first day I met you, through my sickly haze, I thought you might be The One. You walked in and took over my entire life. I'm convinced it was meeting you that made me feel better almost immediately. I've wanted to tell you so many times how I felt but I was afraid to. I thought you would laugh at me. And with Kelly and Lori…" She uncrossed my arms, holding me at arm's length. "I don't want you to say anything right now. Just think about what I've said."

She let go of me then but I could still feel her touching me, still feel her desire for me. There have been very few times in my life where I was left speechless. This was one of them. I looked at her, not knowing what to say, wondering if it could be true. I kept watching her as she turned around and went off to her room. All of my hidden feelings came rushing up to drown me. I tried to fight them off, not willing to think about the possibility of anything happening with Alex. She was unlike any woman I had ever known: independent, strong-willed, with a passion for life that was a little unsettling. And irritating…

CHAPTER THIRTY-FIVE

I liked the new feeling of waking up before the sun without the help of an alarm clock. I enjoyed the feeling of getting a jump on the world even if I was only cheating. With the events of the night before firmly in the front of my mind, I lay in bed, contemplating my next move. I really wished I could turn off the therapist in me. I didn't know what to do next. I was afraid my feelings for Alex were purely physical. I wasn't sure she could live up to her goals of commitment even though she seemed convinced of that herself. I couldn't just jump into bed with her. It wasn't me. I really wanted to see how things turned out with Kelly. I couldn't give up on that without giving it a try. Kelly was caring and serious on our last date and I want to give her the benefit of the doubt. I had made up my mind. There was never going to be anything between me and Alex.

Putting my physical feelings for Alex firmly under lock and key, I got out of bed with a sense of purpose. I went for a jog along the beach. I ran until my breathing became a little worrisome. I don't run very often but, when I do, I wonder why I don't do it more often. I felt drained and exhilarated on the walk back to the house. I picked up coffee and bagels to supplement our selection of fresh fruits.

Alex's room was still dark. I opened up the drapes, let some of the rising sun flood the room and was delighted when Alex rolled over and said, "Could you turn the lights off, please?"

"No. That's the sun, sleepyhead. Wake up. If we're going to Haleakala this morning, we need to get a move on. I'm going to shower. When I get out I expect to see little Alex ready for school." I won't repeat her response. Just know it was incredibly rude and unnecessary.

I came out of the quick shower ready for whatever Alex had planned for me, ready for whatever she wanted to say to me. She was quiet and calm, following me with her eyes, handing me small smiles periodically as we got ready.

"Is there anything you'd like to talk about, Devan?"

"No, not this early. Can we talk about it this evening?"

"Sure."

We hit the road, trying to beat the cloud cover to Haleakala. On the drive up to the volcano, with Alex maneuvering the switchbacks, I thought about what life with Alex would be like. I tried not to, but being so close to her for so long weakened my dawn resolve.

I watched her out of the corner of my eye, concentrating on the nausea-inducing drive, and imagined myself with her. She was beautiful, intelligent, funny and a joy to be around. She was also opinionated, independent and a free spirit. She was intriguing and the thought of spending more time with her filled me with joy. But I refused to be a flavor of the month. I was worth more than a casual encounter. I didn't know how serious Alex had been with her vision of her life in ten years, but I couldn't help but think she wouldn't be able to maintain a long-term relationship. I honestly couldn't see having *anything* serious with Alex, so I couldn't see doing anything with Alex. So, I decided…nothing was going to happen between Alex and me.

We wore more clothing than I thought necessary when we left the house but I was grateful for the warmth on the top of the mountain. Ten thousand feet up can be very cold, even if it is Hawaii. We eventually arrived at the summit, ready to stretch our legs and breathe in thin cold air.

As we warmed up to the day, we began to talk, at first haltingly and then more freely. We stood at the peak and looked down into the crater, marveling at the majesty of nature, loosening our thoughts and tongues. I felt one with nature, a tired cliché, I know, but so true on Maui. I wanted to hold on to something, overwhelmed by my feelings, reaching out to Alex, holding on for the ride. She put her arm around me, sensing I needed the reassurance. We stood like that for a while, until we heard people approach and reluctantly parted. I smile at her and she smiled back, an easy almost shy smile.

We hiked for a while, falling back into an easy, friendly banter, any decisions and serious conversation put on hold. We drove back down the long, winding road, stopping at the welcome center to find trinkets we couldn't live without. I bought my usual two bookmarks. I must have fifty of them at home, and Alex bought me the book, *All About Hawaii*, so when I came back, as she put it "You won't be so touristy." I laughed and longed for the opportunity to come back, stopping myself when I realized I needed to live in the here and now. No sense dreaming of the future when the present was so enjoyable.

Stopping by the house to deposit our bags, we collapsed on the couch for a few minutes of rest before heading out to Kukona's. The couch was small and I couldn't help but sit close to Alex, not quite touching, but close enough to feel her breathing. She reached over and took my hand, weaving her fingers through mine like she had done it a thousand times before. We sat, holding hands, watching TV, until I couldn't take it anymore. She was electric. She was not moving a muscle but still my breathing deepened and I had to open my mouth. This was not going to happen.

I had to stand up and move. I went into the kitchen, over to the refrigerator and looked inside. When I couldn't find anything to do in there, I went over to the sink and rinsed out our coffee cups. I could feel her in the other room, feel her desires and needs. Or maybe I just *thought* I did. I had never been in this situation before, had this connection, real or imaginary, with another woman. I quickly turned around and ran into Alex.

"Please don't be mad at me," Alex said.

"About what?"

Standing inches from me, she placed her hands on my hips. Thank God for squats. I brought my hands up, cupping her face and kissed her. She pulled back and looked at me, questioning my decision, finding her answer. I couldn't stop. The only thing I could do was smile.

She kissed me and every cell in my body remembered her and turned on. I felt myself being pushed back toward my bedroom until I was sitting on the bed looking up at her. Surprised by my boldness, I reached out and gently undid her belt and pulled it out till it fell onto the floor. I undid her jeans and pulled them down till they too fell in a heap on the floor. I reached for the buttons on her shirt and Alex stepped back out of reach.

"Let me. Just watch."

I nodded. She slowly unbuttoned her shirt and let it drop to the floor. She unsnapped her bra and it fell, along with her panties, until the last pieces of her outfit were on the floor. She stood close so I could reach out and touch her. She looked amazing: too muscular to be called thin, too physically beautiful to be called masculine. She was exotic and amazing. Her breasts were small and firm, her stomach flat and defined. Her hips were shapely and her legs were long and lean ending in surprisingly small and dainty feet.

I reached out to touch her and started with her breasts...so soft and delicious. I leaned over to taste a nipple and caressed the other with my fingers. Alex leaned into me and put her hands in my hair. I kept her nipple in my mouth and let my hands roam free. I ran them down her stomach and around to her butt. High and tight. I massaged her for a moment and pulled away from her nipple. I'll be back. I found her eyes watching me.

"Touch me please, Devan."

I brought my hands around to her front and gently eased her legs apart. She had to place her hands on my shoulders. I hoped she'd stay upright. Thankfully, I was sitting when I first felt her wetness on my fingers because I would have fallen. Alex was very wet and ready for me. I moved my fingers back and forth between her lips. She leaned forward and closed her eyes. I found the spot I was looking for and gently pinched her between my thumb and finger. I rubbed back and forth until her breath deepened and she shook slightly. She dug her hands into my shoulders and tried to stay upright. When she came, she yelled out, swayed and fell through me.

"Oh. My. God." She exclaimed on the way down. I wrapped my arms around her, clinging to her beauty.

"I wanted you so badly, I couldn't stand it anymore. You're so beautiful, Alex."

"I know just how you feel. I've wanted you for a very long time." She rolled me over fingering my clothes. "Look. We forgot to take yours off. Here let me."

My clothes came off a lot faster, enough of the foreplay already. When I was naked, she rolled back on top of me and kissed me… no gentleness involved. She reached down to see how ready I was, gasping at my wetness. She kissed her way down my body, stopping briefly at my breasts, before moving on. My breathing slowed and deepened. Was I ready for this? She paused, on her trip down, to look up into my eyes, and to ask me a question I didn't realize I had been waiting my whole life to be asked.

"Can I lick you, Devan?"

I couldn't speak. I grabbed her head and pushed her down, all the time nodding my head. I wanted to scream the first time I felt her tongue on me, but I held it together. I caught the screams in my head. She played with me, licking me until she had me right where she wanted me. I felt the first quiver of my orgasm, familiar and welcome, and then an unfamiliar rush of liquid, fiery pleasure. Words were gone. Thoughts were gone. Just sensations were left. When my orgasm hit, when it rolled over me like a tsunami engulfing all of my senses, my whole body arched, rocked by waves of pleasure. As sensation ebbed, the echoes of a cry reached my ears. My throat was raw. Alex was locked between my legs, her shoulders defending her right to breathe.

"Oh. My. God!" I thought I said. What I heard was an inarticulate jumble.

"I know!" Alex replied from between my legs. "Could you ease up a little so I can breathe?"

"Sorry!" I tried moving my legs, to little effect. "Are my legs still there?"

"Yes, your lovely legs are still attached to your fine ass," she said after crawling up to the head of the bed.

"Are you sure? Because I can't feel them." They must have washed away.

"Come up here with me." Alex helped me to the pillows, helped me get comfortable in my final resting place. Now I could die a happy woman. NOW I see what all the fuss was about. Those tiny "orgasms" I'd had before with Steph? Those clearly left something to be desired. But this? I wanted to take out a full-page ad in the *New York Times* extolling the virtues of Alex's tongue. I wanted to spray-paint my orgasm's rainbow on the face of the moon. I wanted to laugh. I wanted to cry.

"Devan, honey? What are you thinking about?"

"Nothing." No need to say all that out loud. "Why haven't we been doing that since we first met?"

"Because first off that would have been inappropriate in the gym and second you were definitely not ready."

"Good points. I'm ready now."

"Yes. I gathered that." Alex laughed and held me tighter. "You were more than ready. I'm thinking you'll be ready again in the next half hour or so."

"I can't possibly do that again. No way. Not until at least twelve hours have passed. Yeah, tomorrow morning I might be ready again."

"Hmm. I'm thinking that if I go slow," Alex propped herself up on her elbow, "really work you up," she touched her finger to my chin and ran her hand down my stomach, "you could come again tonight."

And she was right. Twice.

CHAPTER THIRTY-SIX

I don't consider myself a deeply religious person, hardly at all really, but I'd said "Oh My God" more in those last twenty-four hours than in the rest of my life combined. And the smiling... my face hurt but I couldn't stop smiling. My throat was raw and other places throbbed. We finally had to order pizza as there was no way we could get dressed and go out amongst Alex's family. At first I didn't want to waste a valuable second spending time inside the house. Now I couldn't leave if I wanted to. We ate propped up in bed, in between rounds, not caring about calories or content. We ate like people who hadn't seen food in days. It was delicious: juicy and tender, fresh and satisfying. I'm not sure if it was the sex or not, but that was damn good pizza.

Everything seemed to have a special glow. The delivery guy had a special aura about him, the food seemed to glow in the box and Alex definitely had a glow about her. I ate my dinner while touching Alex with my foot, afraid if I let her go she would vanish. I wasn't done with her yet. I still had a lot of work to do.

I was the first to wake. I had a hell of a time untangling myself from Alex and the sheets without waking her. It seems we had fallen asleep where we finished last: exhausted, intertwined, happy. Alex was lying on her stomach, face turned away from me, still sleeping. I wanted to jump on her, to squeeze her and tell her my darkest secrets. But I didn't. I wanted to roll her over and demand she tell me what she really wanted from me. But I didn't. I reached my hand out, intent on waking her, unable to contain my feelings for her. But I held back. I was afraid it would be too much for her. I watched her sleep and when that became too much to bear, I lay down next to her, rolling her back toward me. Nothing wrong with a little spooning.

"Hey, babe. What time is it?" she asked, half in this world and half in the sleeping one.

"Let's see. It's ten a.m. Should we shower and go out? I think Kai's supposed to be home soon."

"Do we have to?"

"No. We don't." I rolled her back on her stomach—she looked especially good from this angle—and kissed the lizard on her back.

"That's good. Charlie likes that."

"Charlie?"

"That's what I named my tattoo."

"Really?"

"Yeah, I like to name things."

"Okay, well roll over and you and Charlie stay put. Don't move," I said. "I want to taste you."

She didn't move but she sure did twitch a lot. I prayed she would overlook my inexperience, prayed she wouldn't notice I wasn't very good at this part, prayed she would just pass out and I could tell her about the great time she'd had. I parted her legs with my hands, rubbed her with my fingers, kissed her with my lips. I licked her then, probing with my tongue, taking in her smell and fluids. There are no words. I sucked until she begged me to stop but I wouldn't. I couldn't. She tasted so good. I finally did stop, leaving Alex a pile on the bed, smiling at myself in the mirror as I washed my face.

Looking in the mirror, I saw myself. Who I was and what I wanted was definitely not a surprise. I wanted what everyone else wanted. I wanted to be loved. I wanted to feel like I was the most important person to someone. When I left a room, I wanted the lights to dim, just a little bit, for that one special person in my life. When I came back, I wanted the light to *shine*. Because I mattered. I wanted that someone to be Alex. I couldn't fully comprehend it all while I was still basking in the glow of Maui, but I needed to believe her when she said she thought I was The One. I couldn't go back now, not after what happened. I just hoped she could love me back.

"Devan, come here. I want to touch you."

"I can't. Seriously. I think you are causing damage to vital organs." I wasn't sure about medical terminology but I might have been damaged beyond repair at that point. I leaned against the wall naked, letting her get a good look.

"That sounds like a challenge to me." She smiled and rolled toward me, reaching out for me.

"Don't you dare," I said, and meant it. "I might split right down the middle if you keep it up."

"Okay, okay. I'll go shower." She got up out of bed a little worse for the wear herself. "You stay here and relax."

Relax I will. The bed was warm and inviting. I was hungry but too lazy to make anything. I was thirsty but unwilling to find my water bottle. I guessed I'd just lie there. I must have drifted off to sleep because the next thing I knew Alex was back smelling clean and fresh, kissing me softly on my neck.

"Hmmmm...that feels good."

"I thought you said you couldn't have any more pleasure in your life?"

"Oh yeah. I forgot. Stop doing that."

"Go shower," Alex said. "This is our last day and we need to hit the beach and visit family. Maybe Kai can join us at the beach. You can relax and work on your, um, tan. You really don't tan at all do you?"

"No, but I burn really well."

"Maybe your freckles will grow together one day and you'll be somewhat tan," Alex said.

"I don't hold out hope but I do like the freckles."

"Really? I like them too but a lot of people don't."

"I hated them when I was a kid. I'm not kidding, hated them. But my great-uncle once sat me on his knee, looked at me with a very serious expression, scratched his very bald, completely freckled head and explained the important relationship between freckles and intelligence. It was Uncle Jim who changed my embarrassing freckles into the power source of my intellect."

"Hey. I don't have any freckles!" Alex exclaimed.

"Uncle Jim was a very intelligent man. He knew what he was talking about."

"You redheads…you have all the power don't you?" She stopped and looked closely at my unruly hair. "Your hair seems to be lightening a little. It looks great."

"Take a picture. It will turn dark brown in Washington. It took me years to show any of my natural red after I moved to Texas."

"That's okay. All I have to do is look down to see you are a natural red." She smiled when she said it.

"Stop doing that, please, and help me into the shower. I can't possibly have any more sex today. Just help me up."

"Okay, okay." She laughed and helped me into the shower, closing the door behind her, leaving me alone with my thoughts.

CHAPTER THIRTY-SEVEN

We parked ourselves on the beach in front of the house. When Kai and his girlfriend came back they joined us and we spent the better part of the day in the sand. Alex, Kai and Leilani spent the time swimming and sunning while I watched them from beneath my umbrella. We joined a class of paddle riders. It seemed safer than surfing and I only fell off seven times. Luckily, the water was shallow enough the sand broke my fall most of the time. I blamed Alex for making me a little unsteady. She seemed to be doing just fine, laughing and talking with the others, cruising around me like she had been born on the board. Just looking at her made me smile.

We showered and all piled into the Mustang for the drive over to Kukona's house. We ate chicken, rice, fresh fruit and macaroni salad. We also ate a side of Spam, yes the canned Spam, a favorite of Alex's family. I would really miss them. They made me feel like a cherished part of the family. An unfamiliar sensation. They were open and inviting, something I could get used to very quickly. If only I could take them all back home with me.

I didn't want to think about leaving but was forced to when Alex started packing her things after dinner. We took one last walk along the beach, saying goodbye to the tropical surroundings. We were definitely coming back here again. We had to. Not only was Alex's family here but this was now *our* spot. Our little slice of the world we could look back fondly on as the place we truly came together. Maybe we could come back for our anniversary every year, the same time every year, to celebrate. I needed to slow down. We didn't get married. We had sex, that's all. I didn't want to rush it. I didn't want to be like Ronnie, and run Alex off. She was too important to me.

I took this thought with me back to the room, back with Alex. We went to bed early, making love slowly, taking our time, relishing every moment.

CHAPTER THIRTY-EIGHT

We boarded the plane in Maui with the rest of the happy, carefree passengers, our collective joy spilling out into the aisles. It was a quick four-and-a-half-hour direct flight to Portland. After the movie, we pulled the shades back up and caught our first glimpse of Oregon and its impressive cloud cover. The plane's collective joy faltered, tried to right itself and collapsed in a foggy heap on the jetway. What a shocking return to earth, the impressive tropical views replaced with a cloudy, rainy gray landscape. I tried to hold onto the feeling of Maui, the casual barefoot elegance of the island, but I lost it as I zipped up my parka.

Alex lived in central Vancouver in a cute dark blue-gray Craftsman-style house tucked onto a good-sized lot, a quick fifteen-minute drive from the airport. I was shocked to see a blue hydrangea in the garden on the left side of the house. "Alex! When did you plant that hydrangea?"

She stopped on the sidewalk leading up to the house and put the suitcases down. "Oh, I don't remember. It's been years now.

I planted that when I bought the house because Kukona loved them so much. I wanted her to see it when she came to visit. Why?"

"I was dreaming of blue hydrangeas the morning Steph dumped me and now I'm seeing them everywhere."

"Well, that's a good thing right? Out of the ashes new growth sprouts?"

"I guess so. Maybe I'm just noticing them now. How do you get yours so blue? Corin's is a much lighter blue."

"The pink and the blue hydrangeas are the same plant much like the green and red bell peppers. The hydrangea turns blue when it's planted in slightly acidic soil, which helps absorb the aluminum. That's the key." Alex picked back up her luggage and started for the front door. "Every year I have my picture taken next to the hydrangea to use as my Christmas card. Kukona loves it."

"Why does she love them so much?" We entered her house and put the bags down by the front door.

"She told me once she had a dream of a beautiful woman surrounded by a blue shrub she had never seen before. This woman, she believed, held the key to happiness. The first time she came to visit us, when we were kids, she saw Mom's hydrangea and nearly fainted. She went on and on about that bush, nonstop, the whole trip. Drove Dad nuts!" She laughed at the memory. "Dad would mutter about the crazy woman as he hid in the basement."

"Who was the woman in her dream?"

Alex turned to face me. "She never did say. All she would say was she was a heavenly white woman." Alex turned and disappeared into the hallway.

"Oh."

Her home reflected Alex to a T—it was relaxed, comfortable, bright, airy and filled with carefully placed cherished items. I wanted nothing more than to sit on one of her overstuffed chairs, prop my feet on her coffee table and have a glass of wine, the days of the mai tai now gone. Her kitchen was relatively small, perfect for us non-chefs. I opened the fridge and I had to laugh. The only contents were condiments, beer and a few eggs.

"Alex, where'd you hide the food? That tiny lasagna on the plane didn't do it for me."

Alex leaned into the fridge with me and scratched her chin. "Little food fairies must have broken in and stole it. I swear there was filet mignon, lobster and hundreds of fruits and veggies in here when I left."

"Wow. That would have been delicious. Damn fairies."

"We have two options: order pizza or go out to eat."

"Let's go out. Take me to one of your favorite places." I placed my hand near her heart. "I want to see where you go, what you do."

"Well, we've been to Le Restaurant that's where I normally go but I do like this little Mexican restaurant a few blocks away. They make the *best* cheese enchiladas."

The air felt cold, but it was probably only in the fifties. It just felt like the tundra. The restaurant was tiny, a dozen tables scattered in two small rooms. The exposed red brick made the interior feel warm and cozy. A small bar in the corner housed one of the best mixologists in town Alex informed me and he was not a disappointment. The enchiladas were so good I would probably think about them for days afterward until I couldn't stand it anymore and had to go back. The secret was in the sauce the waitress informed me.

"Did you want to spend the night at my house or should I take you to Linda and Ronnie's?" Alex asked after we had devoured dinner and the bartender Miguel's signature margaritas.

"I just want to be with you, Alex. I don't care where we stay. I do want to go see Corin and Emily, see how they're doing, so why don't we go down to Matt's and then head back to your place and stay there?" Just thinking about getting Alex into bed was enough to deepen the flush on my face brought about by the margaritas.

"Oh baby, don't get me started already." Alex laughed and pulled on her collar. I was making her a little hot and bothered too. "I'd like to see Corin and Emily myself. Make sure, with my own two eyes that they're okay."

"Oh honey, that's one of the many reasons I love you." Oh, crap! I couldn't believe the words had come out of my mouth. Maybe she wouldn't notice.

"What?" Alex asked, being careful not to show any emotions.

"Hmmm? Nothing. Forget it."

"No. Devan, I…"

"You don't have to say anything…"

"But, Devan…"

"It's too early for that. Forget I said it. The margaritas were a little strong for me." She wanted to say something, anything to make me feel better. "Seriously, Alex, don't say a word." I couldn't believe I'd said "I love you." This was how Ronnie had behaved, pushing too hard, too fast. I paid for the meal, rushing to get away from my declaration of love, pulling Alex from the restaurant and back to the house. I was wondering to myself if I really loved her or was I just drunk on sex?

CHAPTER THIRTY-NINE

We found Corin, Sam, Ronnie and Marti over at Matt's. He knew instantly what had transpired in Maui. I don't know if our close proximity gave us away or if we gave off some kind of a signal or what but Matt's sexdar pinged so loud you could see it in his eyes. The slight tension between us gave an impression we were trying to hide something.

"Oh. My. God! Look at you two! I'm so happy for you!" Matt jumped up from the couch, almost knocked over Ronnie, and hugged Alex and me together. "I knew you would hook up. Everybody knew it would happen. Look how cute you two are together. You just glow."

"Okay. Calm down, Matt." Alex seemed little embarrassed by Matt's amusement. "Yes, we're together now. Everyone, just get your little comments out now."

"Devan, what about Kelly?" Ronnie asked. "I thought you were dating her?"

"Yeah, what about Lori?" Marti asked.

"Oh Kelly...right...Lori...well....It was lovely in Maui...I have no willpower..."

Sam commented, "Clearly Kelly and Lori didn't make the cut did they, Devan?"

"No, they didn't," I said, grateful for an end to that conversation. I would have to call them. And my parents who I keep forgetting about.

"Anyway," Marti said, "I'm guessing Maui was a wonderful place?"

"Yes. You have no idea."

"It was an amazing experience," Alex said as she grabbed my hand and held it up to her lips. I snuck a peek at Ronnie, not wanting to stir up any bad feelings from her but I noticed she was smiling a little.

"So, how are you, Corin? Any word on Joe?" I wanted to change the subject of our happiness as I wasn't sure how Ronnie and Linda's relationship was doing at the moment.

"I'm doing a lot better." Corin's damaged arm was protected by a large brace and a lot of padding, strapped to her chest to support it. She was sitting on the edge of the sofa with Sam right next to her. She looked over at Sam who smiled at her.

"We haven't found him yet, Devan." Sam said. "But don't worry we will."

"I hope so. I'd like to relax and go home." I sat on one of the two chairs Matt had facing the couch. Since Marti was sitting in the other chair Alex propped herself on the arm of mine.

"Me too," said Corin.

"I thought we had him a couple days ago, but when we showed up at his mom's house he was nowhere to be found. I swear he had been there recently, just a feeling I had but I'd swear to it," Sam said.

"I have faith you'll catch him, Sam," Marti said.

"Are you leaving me, bestie, now that you have Alex to shack up with?" Ronnie said, from the other end of the couch, with just a little bit of tension in her voice.

"Yes. I don't want to impose on you anymore."

"I'll miss you around the house."

"That reminds me. Where's Emily and Linda?" I just realized I hadn't seen Emily.

"Emily's over at Linda's playing with Cameron," Corin said. "Those two have really hit it off. I was a little worried about letting Emily out of my sight but Sam convinced me Linda would take care of her." Corin patted Sam's arm and left her hand there.

"Linda and I had a little talk and I made sure she had my number. They have two big dogs too," Sam said.

"Linda kicked me out of the house," Ronnie said.

"What!" Marti and I said. Everyone looked over at Ronnie, our eyes wide and shiny.

"Not like that! No, she just suggested, very strongly, I get out of the house for a while."

"Oh, you scared us there for a second," Matt said, patting his chest.

"You guys took that very seriously. You don't think she would actually kick me out of the house. Do you?" Ronnie's eyes had also gotten rather large. She looked over at me. "Devan, is that what you think will happen?"

"No! I don't think so. Probably not." I looked over at Matt for help, who looked over at Marti who looked at the ceiling fan.

"Oh my God. Has it gotten that bad?"

"No, Ronnie," Matt said. "It's just you two seem a little tense recently. That's all."

"He's right," Marti said. "Just a little tense."

"Yeah," Alex chimed in. "Nothing to worry about."

Ronnie looked at each of us, nodded and settled back on the couch. "We definitely need therapy."

"It couldn't hurt," I said. "Therapy works wonders for some people, especially couples. Sometimes we forget relationships need love and attention just like other living things."

"I don't know if I can convince Linda of that but I can try."

"Just tell her you love her and can't imagine the rest of your life without her. Tell her therapy is the way to attain that goal and I'm sure she'll be more than happy to go with you," Corin said. Every head slowly turned toward Corin.

"That's beautiful, Corin," I said.

"Yes, nicely put," Sam said with a smile.

CHAPTER FORTY

The next few weeks went by quickly with work, sex and those crazy things that seem to suck the time right out of your week. Those things like laundry, cooking and general cleaning. I moved in with Alex mostly because Alex insisted I move in. I almost forgot my declaration of love, neither of us mentioning it, neither of us wanting to bring it up, fearing how the other would react. I went to the gym after work most days, working out with Alex when she could and following her home where we helped each other shower. We ate out, cooked together at home, did couples things like the Portland Zoo and various museums, saw several movies and went to my new favorite ice cream shop on Main Street.

One day after work, I went to the gym and found Alex missing. Ashley the friendly fit girl Alex had hired to help her was alone at the front counter.

"Come to see Alex?"

"Maybe I came to see you."

"I doubt that," she said with a smile. "Although, if you looked at me the way you look at Alex, I'd like that."

"Am I that obvious?"

"Oh yeah. But don't worry. It's nice to see."

"Where is Alex, by the way?"

"She said she had something to take care of for a couple of hours. She wanted you to know she would probably be back before you finished your workout but if she doesn't make it back in time just hang out here until she gets back." Ashley was reading the notes Alex had left for her. "She wanted me to get this right."

"I don't feel like doing much of anything today so I think I'll stop by Marcozi's Deli on the way home and pick up a sandwich for dinner. Just tell Alex I'll be at home waiting for her and I'll try and save her half a sandwich."

I drove over to Main Street to the little deli we like so much to order a meatball sandwich to go, not something I would order every day but a delicious treat I ordered on days I was feeling out of sorts and tired. I saw them, out of the corner of my eye, while I was sitting at a table waiting for my sandwich. I saw Cathy first and almost yelled across the street to her.

The greeting died in my throat when Cathy turned around and grabbed Alex's arm. They were standing in front of an apartment building and Alex had just put her jacket back on. Cathy handed Alex a key and Alex closed her hand around it. She looked down at the key, laughed, shook her head and said something to Cathy. Cathy leaned into her and kissed her, pressing her body up against Alex's. Alex folded her arms around Cathy, and they held the grasp for what seemed like an eternity.

I looked away. I couldn't watch it anymore. That's when the bad feeling in my stomach, the one I'd been carrying around all day, fully blossomed and took over. My order was up and I stood, the sandwich I wouldn't be able to eat clutched in my hand, my eyes unable to leave Cathy and Alex. They were deep in conversation, a look of tenderness on Alex's face I wouldn't be able to forget and it dawned on me what was happening. This was the end for Alex and me. For *me* our relationship had just begun but for Alex it was already old and worn-out.

How could I have been such a fool? Why was I so surprised? I *knew* how she was *before* I jumped willingly in to bed with her. I wanted to go over to them, throw my sandwich at them and yell until I was hoarse.

But I didn't. I went to see Linda instead. I handed my sandwich to her. She gave me a look but didn't say a word and I went into the basement and sat on the bed too much of a wreck to cry. Had I pushed her into her behavior with my attitude and declaration of love?

I didn't go up to see her when I heard her upstairs. I was hurting too much. Alex came to the top of the stairs and said, "Devan, are you okay? Linda says you're upset."

"Go away. Leave me alone. I mean it." It felt like I had spat the words out and I must have because Alex didn't come down.

Steph had hurt me when she left but it was *nothing* compared to what I felt about Alex and Cathy. I felt like Alex had positioned me for a beautiful picture, promising it would be the best shot ever taken, putting me just where she wanted me, then she got into her car and backed over me. I was left with a feeling of utter disbelief and my body hurt all over. My heart seemed to have shriveled in my chest and died.

With Steph, it had been different. Steph hurt my feelings when she left, hurt my pride when she chose someone else. I realized now that I *really* loved Alex. But I *never* should have gone to Maui with her. The tropical breezes and mai tais caused my moral compass to falter. I had convinced myself our relationship was different. I had been certain Alex and I were in love, a long-lasting love which would only end with death do us part.

I spent the night by myself down in the basement without eating or talking with anyone. I mostly sat with my back against the wall with my legs pulled firmly to my chest crying and feeling sorry for myself. I knew how Alex was *before* we went to Maui, that she was a player. And yet I still found myself alone, curled up into a ball crying at the loneliness engulfing me. I'd always thought of myself as above average in intelligence but not anymore. How could I have been so dumb?

I woke up early, at least I *think* it was early. Someone had come down at some point and covered me with a blanket because I had been unable to crawl under the covers. I wanted to call in sick. I knew that wouldn't help so I got ready for work in a haze of grief. I was thankful I still had some stuff left at Linda and Ronnie's. I headed up the stairs for the door, building myself up for the day, unable to forget the image of Cathy and Alex. I had to move on, had to power on through the day, had to put Alex behind me.

Alex was waiting for me in the kitchen looking confused and tired, panicked and lonely. We were alone, everyone else in the house hiding in the far corners.

"What the hell is going on, Devan?" Alex asked. She looked very uncomfortable, like she knew what I was going to say and wanted nothing to do with that conversation.

"I saw you with Cathy yesterday," I replied.

"And...?"

"You looked very cozy together. As a matter of fact you had that look on your face, the one you have after sex." My anger rose at the memory.

"Cathy and I went out for a drink. So?" Alex sounded a little defensive. "We're old friends who occasionally get together and talk. There's nothing wrong with that." I felt she was holding something back, a *big* something.

"It looked a little more intimate than that, Alex." I crossed my arms in front of my chest. "And we both know you and Cathy do more than meet for the occasional beer."

"You can't do this, Devan. You have to believe me when I tell you. Nothing happened between Cathy and me. I can't help it if you don't believe me."

"You're right, Alex. You can't help it." I walked around her, out the door and to my car. I couldn't believe it had ended like this. Just the day before I was happier than I'd been since I was a child and my dad introduced me to caramel apples. How could it have become so bad so quickly? With Steph it was never really *good* so I think I was mostly surprised she had the balls to leave first. But Alex and me, *that* had been good. I let myself believe I had met the one for me...that our relationship would be written up in the papers on our fiftieth anniversary (I knew that fifty years hence, it would be common for lesbian couples to celebrate their long-term relationships publicly).

* * *

When I got to Linda and Ronnie's that evening, after a long day of putting off Linda's gentle questions, I found an envelope on the kitchen table. It was from Alex. I couldn't bear to read it because I knew this was my "Dear Devan" letter. She was probably very kind and loveable in our break up letter along the lines of "These things just don't work out sometimes, just know I still care about you." Ronnie was right. It hadn't ended well for me. It was ending rather badly for me. I put the letter in my back pocket, deciding I would read it after a drink or two at home. I needed to go back to my own apartment and be alone for a little while. There were too many kind and intrigued souls in this house. I needed some time alone to think.

CHAPTER FORTY-ONE

I parked in the back, near the stairs and went up into my apartment for the first time since the attack. I went to use the bathroom and when I came out I found Steiner standing in the middle of my apartment, his right hand casually laid on the couch, waiting for me. At least he let me finish.

"Hi there," Steiner said as his lips peeled back from his ugly teeth in an attempt to smile.

"Corin's safe," I said, trying to sound strong.

"I came here to see you. I'll visit her later."

Oh shit. I was all alone. I needed to stay focused and think about our self-defense training. I told myself not to panic. I wanted to survive. I remembered my pepper spray was in my bag. *Over by the front door*. Behind Steiner. The kitchen was to my left. If I got a jump on him, the couch would block his path to the kitchen. Steiner was too big and strong for me.

"Get out."

"Why would I do that? I've been waiting for this moment a long time. I've been following you everywhere since I saw you at that faggot's house. I've just been waiting for the right moment to visit you."

He slowly reached up to take off his jacket and I made a run for the kitchen. I guess he was momentarily stunned, giving me three or four steps on him. I angled for the left-hand side of the kitchen. The side with the knives. He moved too quickly and I picked up the whole *block* of knives, swung around and aimed for his face. He reached up with his arm and deflected most of the blow. The corner of the block hit him near his right eye and I pushed with all my might. He staggered to his left and I screamed and ran for the front door.

Steiner stumbled but still caught me before I made it to the door. He pushed me into it and I bounced off and fell on my purse.

"You bitch!" He pulled his leg back to kick me and I rolled over, grabbed the pepper spray and was backed up against the door. His kick caught me in my solar plexus and I almost let go of the spray. The pain came quickly, sucking all the air out of my lungs. Steiner picked me up, slammed me against the door and I brought my spray up and unloaded on him.

"Shit!" Steiner's hands flew to his face and he took a step back. "Motherfucker!"

I squatted down and drove my head up into his jaw. He fell to the floor, holding his face, moaning and rolling on the floor. I whirled around, whipped open the door and almost ran into Sam, who was running up the stairs.

"Sam!" I flung myself at her, grateful she had a hand on the railing or we both would have gone over. Her other hand was holding her gun. I hugged her and refused to let go.

"Devan! What's going on? I heard yelling." She didn't put her gun away but pointed it down and away.

"Steiner." The adrenaline was still pumping through my body and Sam couldn't untangle herself from me.

"Devan, let go and let me see. Please."

I let go just enough and Sam went through the open door. I heard sirens in the distance and I started to shake. I took a deep breath and walked into the apartment as Sam was cuffing Steiner.

"Do. Not. Move. Steiner," she said when he started squirming. "Devan, go outside and wait please."

"No. I will not let him destroy the sanctity of my home," I said as I sank onto the couch. The other officers arrived and an ambulance was called. I wasn't physically injured, except for a slight headache and a soon-to-be nasty bruise on my chest, so when they looked me over they told me I was good to go. After Steiner had been chained to a gurney and carted off to the hospital, glaring at Sam the whole time, Sam came and crouched next to me, putting her hand on my knee.

"Can I get you anything?"

"In the cupboard above the fridge. With a shot glass please." Sam brought me the Jack Daniels, poured a shot and handed it to me.

"Can you keep it down?"

"I think so." I let the liquid seep into the far corners of my body. Then I walked over to the sink and threw up. I gripped the counter, washed out my mouth and sat back down. I stuck the glass out toward her. "One more please." There. I felt better.

"I'm not so worried about you now. You haven't forgotten your manners." Sam smiled and I felt even better. She placed the Jack Daniels on the table near me.

"Did Steiner set off the alarm when he broke in, Sam? Is that how you were outside?"

"No, the alarm seems to be off. And the door doesn't look damaged. Did you lock the door when you came in, Devan?"

"Um…I think so?"

"Think so, huh? No, I try and come around once a day to see how things look. I saw your car and wanted to see what you were doing here. I heard you scream and made a run for it."

"Thank you, Sam."

"You're welcome. Anyone you want me to call?" She lifted up her eyebrows waiting for my response. I hesitated. Did I want to call Alex? "It's okay, Devan. Let me go talk with Burkov. I'll be right back."

I sat on my couch, in my apartment, the bitter taste of fear gone, the adrenaline gone, the shaking gone. I fell asleep. I was awakened by two hands carefully placed on my thighs. I tensed up and my eyes flew open.

"It's me, honey. Alex." Alex was on her knees in front of me, looking worried and worn down. "Baby, what happened?"

I cried and Alex gathered me in her arms, holding me until I couldn't cry any more. "Don't worry. You don't have to say anything."

"Why are you here?" I didn't want to see Alex when I felt this vulnerable. I just wanted to be left alone. I did feel safer, now that she was here.

"Sam called me. Told me you kicked Steiner's ass again. Broke his jaw. That's my girl," Alex said still holding me loosely in her arms. Sam came back in and gently told us we could leave. But I didn't want to leave. This was my home. Alex moved next to me on the couch and asked me what I wanted to do.

"I want you to take me to see Corin. I want to tell her, in person, what happened." I wanted to tell her we got him. That he was going to rot in jail.

"That would mean you would have to leave the sanctity of your home, Devan." Sam said with what I thought was a whisper of a smile.

"Oh. Right."

"I won't tell anyone if you don't. You should definitely drive, Alex."

"Okay." Alex helped me down to the car and drove me over to Matt's. I walked in ahead of Alex and found Corin in the kitchen. She knew right away something was wrong.

"What happened? Are you okay, Devan?" She looked me over, checking for blood.

"He's been arrested, Corin. You're safe now." I started to cry, not from fear and anxiety but from relief and joy. Corin carefully came around the table, holding her injured arm close to her chest, stopping in front of me.

"You're kidding."

"Would I kid about that?"

"No." She thought about it. "No, I guess you wouldn't." She looked me square in the eye and, with a quivering bottom lip, said, "I'm so sorry, Devan. This is entirely my fault. If I hadn't…"

"Stop." I wouldn't let her finish that thought. "This is in no way your fault and let me say that again just in case you missed it the first time...this is in no way your fault, Corin. This is Joe Steiner's fault. All of us here are innocent bystanders. This is all Steiner's fault, Corin, and I don't ever want to hear you apologize for something that asshole has done. Am I clear?"

"Yes."

"Whose fault is it?" I asked because I had to hear her say it.

"This is Steiner's fault," she said. And then she hugged me. Well, that made me cry even harder. We held each other and cried.

Emily came into the kitchen and asked us what was wrong.

"Nothing's wrong, honey. We're happy," Corin said.

"So you cry when you're happy too?"

"Yes, sometimes adults cry when they're happy too," I explained.

"Oh, I don't think I want to be an adult," Emily said and wandered out of the kitchen. We all had a good laugh about that one. Laughed so hard we cried.

CHAPTER FORTY-TWO

Alex drove me back home. I didn't want her to leave me but I couldn't stand her being so close. She directed me toward the couch and I sat, grateful for a soft landing.

"Can I stay with you tonight, Devan?" She was almost pleading with me.

"I don't know, Alex. I…"

"Did you read my letter?"

I leaned back on the couch and said, "What letter?"

"The letter I left for you at Linda and Ronnie's. I wanted to tell you in person but I couldn't reach you."

"Oh that letter. I've been a little busy." I reached around to my back pocket where Alex's letter had been along for the ride, wincing at the pain in my chest. The envelope was a little crumpled.

"Read it."

"I can't focus. You read it." Alex took the letter and gently flattened it along my thigh, trying to get the wrinkles out. She cleared her throat, gave me a little embarrassed grin and began.

Dear Devan,

I'm sorry you got the wrong impression the other night. Cathy and I slept together in the past. I can't deny that fact. But we have NOT slept together since you and I became a couple. I love you too, Devan. I went to talk with Cathy and give her back her spare key. Her response to stress is to jump into bed with someone and she thought that someone was me. She was mistaken. She tried to give me back the key and I laughed at her determination. She kissed me and caught me momentarily off guard. We have shared a lot over the years. That part of my life is over. I can't change my history but I can create a new one.

I was telling her how happy you made me. The look on my face was the love I feel for you, Devan. I love you. Please believe me and let me spend the rest of my life proving to you just how much I love you.

I heard this story, from a very good friend of mine, about a recent breakup...well, I won't bore you with the details, you've probably heard this one before...let me just tell you it gave me an idea:

If I intertwine your heart with mine
If I make it so you can't see up/down/left/right
Without seeing/feeling/breathing/knowing me
You will never leave.
That way I can toy with you here/there/everywhere
And you can't get away
Because your heart will be mine.
Do you see my diabolical plan?
And then when you're not looking
We will live/breathe/grow old together and you will not realize it and neither will I
Because my heart will be yours.

Of course, I have a lot of work to do, but I like my plan. It's not original, no, but I like the way mine ends. Kukona explained to me, our first night in Maui, how you were the woman she dreamed about that night all those years ago, the woman who was the key to happiness. The key to my happiness, it turns out. You are the woman in the blue hydrangeas. I believe this completely now and I will spend the rest of my life loving you. Kukona is never wrong. Please come find me.

Yours for as long as you will have me,

Alex

Oh, she's good. Knows just how to make me cry. I gathered her up in my arms and we hugged until I had to see her face, had to look into her eyes. I saw her love for me and I realized she would never hurt me. That was what love looked like.

"I love you, baby," Alex said.

"I love you too," I said. And we kissed.